TWO OLDE DRAGONS WRITING WYRD STORIES

An Anthology

www.YeOldeDragonBooks.com

Ye Olde Dragon Books
P.O. Box 30802
Middleburg Hts., OH 44130

www.YeOldeDragonBooks.com

2OldeDragons@gmail.com

FOREWORD

Dragons! They shimmer with gleaming scales, iridescent in the sunlight. They mesmerize us, they scare us, they awe us. We see them as defenders like *Dragonheart*, or as devourers like the dragons in *Reign of Fire*. We want our own pets like Daenerys on *Game of Thrones*, yet we fear them as Jon Snow and Tyrion Lanister did. We wish for one like *Pete's Dragon*, who will keep us safe, but we fear the fire-breathing, burn-a-knight-to-a-crisp variety. We buy statues to put in our gardens, pictures to hang on our walls.

Michelle and I love dragons, as do most fantasy writers. We took them as our logo, bought tee shirts, and costumes, and all manner of dragon-ish swag for our publishing house.

What we needed were dragon *stories*.

So here they are. Four stories straight from the mouths of the Two Olde Dragons themselves. We didn't plan it out. But what we ended up with takes you from the old days in our history, legendary days gone by, to a modern horror story, and finally a futuristic space adventure. We bring you a full range to enjoy in one small book!

But as every dragon knows, tales like these need a Bard, someone to sing the songs of dragons, to put the tales to music and spread the legends far and wide. Enter my old friend, James K. Bowers. Many, many moons ago, Jim plucked me out of my little niche of poetry and devotional writing and dropped me headlong into the world of science fiction and fantasy. I became so enthralled with the worlds I discovered, I never left. It only seems right that he should be our Bard, with two extraordinary poems about dragons, epic pieces that deserve a much wider audience than our small writing group.

Without further ado, welcome to the Dragon's Den. We don't bite, but we do serve tea.

Enjoy your stay!

Deborah Cullins Smith
June 2021

Please feel free to visit our website and browse, read blog posts, learn about our different titles, and yield -- yield, please! -- to temptation…

The month before a new book is released, that title will be available from our storefront (before anywhere else online) for $1 off, in both paper and ebook. We have just launched what we hope will be a long-running series of anthologies. The spring will have a fairytale theme, and in the fall, a classic movie monster theme. Plus you can always check out the many dragons up for "adoption," hand-made, every one unique.

Thanks for reading, and please come by soon!

www.YeOldeDragonBooks.com

Table of Contents

DRAGONBANE
By James K. Bowers

'Tis sung in minstrel's ballads in bittersweet refrains --
    Grim rime born of Fortune's jest -- the Song of Dragonbane:
Once bathed in regal splendours, the castle stood in pride,
    But now just lay abandoned, all cares and hopes denied.
No monks pray in the chapel, no criers mark the hours.
    No merchants fill the market square, no archers man the towers.
Gone the lowly chambermaids, the deacons and the lords;
    Gone, too, the maids-in-waiting and knights with shining
swords.
Away have fled the armigers, the stewards and the squires;
    The bailey stands unguarded, no pennants grace the spires.
The smithy's forge knows not flame; the wellsprings all are dry;
    No hearthfires fend December; no gardens greet July.
No torches brighten chambers, nor light forgotten halls;
    Winds moan their hollow dirges past cracked and tumbled
walls.
The emptiness resounding screams sadness all the more,
    For the innocence of youth is now Misfortune's whore.
Deep within the mould'ring keep, 'midst the ruin and the dust,
    Rests the blade of blackest lore, now cloaked in sanguine rust.
Once proudly borne in battle, this sword did glory gain,
    Before men knew its secrets and named it Dragonbane.
Know this sword is more than steel, and wrought by more than fire.
    Know, too, this sword is heartless, with death its lone desire.
Its soul arose and wakened from hauteur and from spite,
    From magics gleaned from dragon's blood, from ice, and winter
night.
A maiden's heart, a fallen tear, a warrior's iron nerves --
    Victims of the hell-forged blade to feed the curse it serves.
By this sword was Honor slain, then Faith and Gallantry;
    And struck dead in the carnage, lay golden Chivalry.
So fled bold knights and heroes, far from the frightful spawn,

Seeking solace from the distance of elsewhen's brighter dawn.
Though dream some fools and reavers, of power, wealth, and fame,
  Not one dares venture northward, the blacksouled sword to
claim,
For there within the castle walls, an old man struggles still
  To break the spell of evil, his destiny to fill.
Within the hall of feasting, now open to the sky,
  He stands in silent vigil, unmoved as time goes by.
He watches o'er the maiden, her lifeless form now bone,
  Beside the sword so dreadful, upon the timeworn stone.
Days pass by and so, too, nights, and seasons become years;
  He kneels, he whispers gently, and sheds his somber tears.
His breath is short and labored, his sinews stiff and weak;
  His bones are old and brittle, mere memories of his peak.
Against the Curse alone he stands, beneath grey-shrouded skies,
  And wields his sword of promise, of hope, and summer sighs.
His armor is his courage, his shield his heart of glass,
  Yet though he battles bravely, he cannot change his past.
Some say on lonely winter nights, when all is cold and clear,
  The warrior, old and feeble, sobs prayers through sorrow's
tears,
And when perchance he listens, he hears a dragon's roar --
  From long ago it echoes to touch his heart once more.
It brings him grief and sorrow, and heralds fitful sleep,
  With dreams of errant ventures and of this woeful keep:
He finds himself much younger, much stronger, yet unwise,
  And cannot end the nightmare, no matter how he tries.
He dreams of knighthood questing, and vanquishing a foe.
  He dreams of knighthood dying that night so long ago.
In slumber's dark embracing, he journeys back those years
  To fight again the dragon, to shed again his tears.
He feels his sword strike cleanly; he hears her dying breath;
  He sees the truth now clearly: 'twas he who welcomed death.
He holds again the maiden, and brushes back her hair,
  Again he begs the angels her life to somehow spare.
Then from the dream he wakens, and stares across the room;
  There he sees no miracle to free him from this doom.
Within her cave of crystal, her lair of evergleams,
  Nevermore will dragon sleep -- his sundered spirit screams:
"Weep not, O fair young maidens, shed not your tears in vain.

Pity not this tortured soul who wielded Dragonbane..."

Written in 1994 and published in Kankakee Community College's
The Prairie Fire, 1995.

THE DRAGON EGG
By Deborah Cullins Smith

"Mine! All mine!" Jasmine giggled as she ran a gentle fingertip over the rough surface of the enormous orb. Dragon eggs were incredibly rare, and she really shouldn't have stolen it. The mama dragon might become just a tad cranky, but seven-year old Jasmine banked on the hope that perhaps dragons couldn't count. The nest still contained three golden-red eggs. Surely three baby dragons would be enough to keep the mama busy.

A shiver raced up and down Jasmine's spine. Retribution would be swift and brutal if the mama reptile chose to vent her wrath. But Jasmine pushed those thoughts down. She had a plan, and nothing was going to stand in her way.

"Maybe," Jasmine whispered to the egg, "if I raise you as my very own baby, you won't become mean like the others. You could even protect us from your brothers and sisters."

She nodded, smiling brightly at the image that flashed in her mind. The whole village would clap and cheer as her dragon glared angrily and bared its teeth at other intrusive monsters. Those bad dragons would screech and flee in terror when they saw her astride the back of her personal guardian! She would love him, feed him, then train him when he grew older. Once the tribal leaders saw what she had accomplished, they couldn't possibly be mad over one little dragon egg — one little broken rule.

Jasmine had heard it all her life. The laws for their village were simple.

Take care of one another, and protect your neighbors.
Share with those who are in need.
Never steal.
Never kill, except to provide meat for your family.
Honor the Elders and obey their directives.
Provide for the widows and orphans.
And never, never harbor a dragon's egg.
If you find a dragon's nest, you must report it to the village elders

immediately.

For the most part, dragons left them alone, but if one chose to nest too near the village, it had to be "dealt with" before the dragonets could hatch. That meant killing the mother and destroying the eggs. Jasmine sniffed at the thought.

"What about not killing? Dragons are not used for meat, so doesn't that mean we aren't supposed to kill them?" To her seven-year-old mind, that was a logical conclusion.

For a brief moment, Jasmine blanched at the formidable visage of her mother towering over her, angry creases deepening between fierce eyebrows. But she raised her chin in defiance and the fearsome phantom vanished.

Jasmine patted her egg and fluffed the nest of soft moss and leaves she had gathered to cradle her treasure. The grotto was her secret hideaway, the one place in the world where she could escape the scolding of the adults. It lay deep in the forest, far from prying eyes, where she would be able to hatch her egg in safety. Jasmine often brought wounded animals or orphans to her grotto and nursed them tenderly until they were well enough or mature enough to survive on their own. A small brook burbled gently nearby and sweet berries grew in abundance along its banks. It was an ideal haven. The stone walls of the grotto formed a small shelter and she had pushed the nest toward the back wall, as she remembered other times and injured, needy animals.

Once it was a clutch of baby rabbits. The mother had been shot by some of the boys in the village who had been hunting with their bows and arrows. While they crowed over a perfect head shot, Jasmine had slipped through the underbrush and found the orphans. She waited until the boys returned home before she moved the nest to her grotto by carrying them in the hem of her dress. They eventually left the nest. She hoped they still survived out in the forest somewhere, and had not ended up in someone's soup pot.

Then there had been three baby sparrows, knocked from their nest. Two died, despite her tender ministrations, but one had finally flown from her grotto. Her heart had all but burst with pride as it took to the trees.

She'd been hard pressed to explain the bloody little teeth marks on her fingers when she had rescued a young fox from her father's traps, but she, too, had gradually come to trust Jasmine enough to allow the girl to tend her wounded foreleg. Before long, the little fox had dashed away, stopping only once to blink her large brown eyes at the human who had saved her life.

Then today, she'd spied the nest. Four big eggs nestled together in a bed of moss and leaves. The mama dragon was nowhere to be seen. The golden-red orbs had glimmered in the sunlight. In her mind, Jasmine heard Elder Andrew telling them for the umpteenth time, *"Never harbor a dragon egg."* She chewed her lip. But it was so pretty!

What if… She ran a gamut of possibilities. She'd often wondered what made a dragon so bad. Maybe the mothers were to blame. Maybe they trained their dragonets to be mean to people. (After all, her own relationship with her mother was fractious at best!) What if a dragonet was raised by a human? Trained to be gentle with people? Wouldn't that make a difference in how a dragon turned out in the end?

Elder Andrew's words haunted her again. *"Never harbor a dragon egg!"*

Everyone did what Elder Andrew told them to. Jasmine wondered why that was. Certainly, he was considered wise, but what if… What if Elder Andrew was wrong about dragons? She'd dealt with wild animals before. Why should a dragon be so different?

Sure, a grown dragon was nothing to play around with. But a baby dragonet! That might be a different story entirely. What if she could train a dragonet, then present it to the village as her pet? Or better yet, what if it could protect her? Protect the entire village! Wouldn't that be a wonderful thing? Then maybe people would stop killing off the dragons. At least the baby ones. They might one day have a whole herd of dragons to protect their village!

A shrill screech had split the air while she daydreamed. The dragon was returning! Jasmine had hesitated for only a second before she reached out and grabbed one of the eggs with both hands. Cradling it carefully in her apron, and holding it tightly against her body, she turned and ran through the woods until she had reached her secret grotto.

~~~~~

She patted the moss once again and leaned her face against the rough shell of the dragon egg.

"We shall be great friends, you and I," she whispered, stroking
~~~~~

the egg gently. "But for now, I must go home or they'll come looking for me."

~~~~~

The next day, she slipped into the grotto. Her legs stung from the willow branch her mother had used to punish her for dropping and breaking her best meat platter, and tears had gathered in her eyes. It was always something with her mother.

"Jasmine! You shouldn't wander off like that. What if raiders came through the village? What if you are attacked by a wild animal? I can't protect you if I can't find you."

"Jasmine! Just look at your gown. Another tear. Do you think cloth grows on trees?"

"Jasmine! You've stepped on your father's new plantlings. Do you want to ruin the garden? What will we eat this winter without a harvest?"

She turned to the egg to pour out her sorrows and gasped. The egg rattled and a hairline crack appeared along the top.

"So soon?" she whispered. She reached out eager fingertips toward the egg, and jerked back in surprise when the egg rattled again. The crack became a fissure that widened from top to bottom. Tiny claws appeared at the edge of the crack, and Jasmine forgot to breathe as she witnessed a new life form emerging from its shell. An eye peeked out at her and a soft cheep echoed against the stone walls of the grotto.

"Come on, my little darling," she cooed. "Come on out."

One golden eyeball blinked, then stared at Jasmine as a greenish-brown snout poked through the shell. Another squawk revealed a row of sharp little teeth and the creature pushed his head completely out, revealing his second golden eye and spikes along the top of his head. His curiosity matched Jasmine's awe as they stared at one another.

Jasmine's finger petted the tiny head, and discovered that the spikes were soft and tickled her knuckles. She giggled and touched the small snout. The dragonet nosed against her hand and chittered softly. She giggled again.

"I'll call you-u-u-u-u…" She thought hard for an appropriate name. "Giggles?" She shook her golden curls. "Not scary enough. No one will believe our village is protected by a dragon named Giggles." She thought again. "What abo-o-o-o-out… Incense? You'll burn up other dragons and save us. No, no, no. That's not right either."
~~~~~

Her frown deepened as she pondered her dilemma.

"I know!" she exclaimed as her eyes lit up and she clapped her hands in delight. "Lightfire! Because you'll light up the skies—once you learn to fly, that is," she amended quickly. "Besides, you are a dragon and your name must sound grand, for you will be the biggest and the best."

The baby dragon shook off the remnants of his shell and flopped on the ground in front of Jasmine, wings outspread on the mossy bed.

Jasmine scurried to the brook and picked a handful of berries, which she fed to the tiny creature one at a time. It pecked at two berries, then its eyes drooped wearily.

"Poor baby," murmured Jasmine. "Being born is hard work, isn't it?"

She removed a few of the egg shells from the moss and placed a handful of berries nearby.

"You can eat these until I can come back to feed you again," she said, petting the tiny head gently.

~~~~~

Jasmine faced another scolding for disappearing again, but she considered it a small price to pay for the secret she held so near to her young heart. She took her punishment meekly and still managed to sneak away one more time before bed to check on Lightfire.

The little dragon chirped a greeting, and climbed willingly into Jasmine's lap. The little girl cooed and cuddled him, took him to the brook for a drink of water, and picked another handful of berries to feast on until morning. Then she tucked the dragonet back into the moss in the grotto and hurried home.

"Jasmine, you really must stop running off by yourself," her father said after her mother had railed at her once again. "Don't you know how much your mama loves you? You scare her when you disappear like that."

"She doesn't love me," she mumbled, curling up in his lap as he sat in the old oak rocking chair before the fireplace.

"Yes, she does, chick-a-dee," he said, stroking her curls. His touch was gentle, but his voice was firm. "Someday maybe you'll understand how much she loves you. But for now, you have to try to obey her."

Why does everyone think obedience is such a big deal? She sighed.

"To bed, Jasmine." Her mother's voice still carried a note of
~~~~~

anger.

"Go," her father whispered. "Tomorrow will be better."

Jasmine highly doubted that, but she kissed her father's cheek, smiling as his beard tickled her nose. Skirting widely around her mother's rigid form, she climbed the ladder to the loft and snuggled beneath her quilt in the small bed. She could hear the words between her parents, though they tried to keep their voices low.

"She's just a child, Lizzie," her father reasoned. "She doesn't understand the dangers in the woods. Most of the village children roam freely, and you know it. Rarely do we have problems."

"But what if she runs into wild animals?" Her mother's distraught whispers filtered up the rickety stairs.

"Then God help the animals!" Her father's laughter sounded muffled.

"William, I mean it. She's only seven this year. She isn't wise enough to be in the woods…"

"Lizzie, you know you were the same way when you were young! We grew up together. How many times did you ask my help with this animal or that? She's just like you, my dear wife!"

Jasmine pondered that. Just like her mother? *Her* mother? Did she really try to heal the wild animals too? Then why couldn't she understand the need to go into the forest alone? She flipped to her side and wondered what her mother had been like as a child. No, there was no way they had anything in common! They were so different. She rolled to her back and stared at the ceiling. Her mother was so demanding, so strict. She heard the patter of rain tapping softly on the timbers above her head. Her eyelids drooped, and she rolled to her side once again before falling asleep.

~~~~~

"Wake up, Jasmine! You must run and hide!" Mother's voice pulled Jasmine from a lovely dream in the middle of the night. It was followed by an inhuman shrieking and the screams of the villagers.

She heard the mournful sound of the alarm horns. Watchmen only blew the horns when there was danger. Jasmine's stomach flip-flopped. Danger of a dragon!

Jasmine ran from her home, her small hand clinging to her mother's larger one. A glance over her shoulder revealed an angry female dragon unleashing blast after blast of hot, fetid fire as she swooped over the village time after time. Thatch roofs burst into flames and the women and children ran for the trees where they
~~~~~

could hide. The men shot arrows and threw spears, but nothing seemed to stop the raging fury in the night sky. A lucky slice by Elder Andrew's sword ripped through the beast's right wing, and a volley of arrows finally pierced her breast as the dragon plummeted to the ground. Three of the strongest men in the village took axes to the body of the dragon, while the rest of the village began dousing the flames to save what structures they could.

Jasmine watched the destruction in horror. *Did I cause this?* She wondered about it, then brushed the thoughts away like mosquitos in summer. *She should have stayed with her other three eggs,* she thought. *It was stupid of her to attack our village.*

As the all clear was given, the women and children crept back out of the woods to join the men. They drew bucket after bucket of water from the well and finally mastered the fires.

"What could have caused that dragon to attack us?" Clarissa, the blacksmith's wife, asked the cluster of women at the well.

"Our people have not encroached on a dragon's territory for some eight summers now," whined another plump villager.

"Nay, 'tis only been five summers," objected Dinara, the tanner's wife. "Remember the year when young Phillip tried to steal a dragon's egg? None has dared venture near the mountainside since."

Jasmine felt the blood drain from her face and was thankful for the darkness of the night, which hid her expression. She didn't know any boys named Phillip, so she wondered what had happened to him. She would have only been two years old at the time. But how could she ask about the boy without raising questions that she didn't want to answer? Jasmine glanced at her mother, then quickly away again, as she saw those sharp maternal eyes searching her trembling soul.

~~~~~

Surely, she would not, Lizzie thought. But she did not ask the questions that might reveal her daughter's guilt in the matter. If William was right, Jasmine most likely had hiding places in the woods. But not even she would be foolish enough to play with a dragon's fire… Would she? Lizzie trembled. Perhaps William could talk to Jasmine later. When things calmed down again. He seemed to relate to the girl better than she did. *We're too much alike.* The thought did not comfort her.

~~~~~

Elder Andrew stood in the center of the village, his face

blackened with soot, his sword resting flat on his shoulder. "Brethren, are your families accounted for? What injuries are there?"

"My wife was trapped in our house when the dragon attacked," called the tavern owner, Benjamin. "She has some burns on her arms."

Elder Andrew nodded to the midwife, Mistress Fiona, who also tended to most of the village's medical needs. She turned toward the tavern to care for the woman.

"My son took a bad fall. He tried to climb the tree by our house to douse the fire in the thatch. I think his leg may be broken." This from the man who owned the local dairy. Mistress Fiona stopped in mid-stride.

"If you have wounded, bring them to the tavern. I can't run all over the village tonight. I'll treat everyone from there," she said loudly, nodding toward Elder Andrew.

"Aye, you heard Mistress Fiona," the elder said. "Bring your wounded to the tavern." He glanced at Benjamin and received acceptance of the burden without hesitation.

"With your permission, Elder Andrew, I'll head home to help," Benjamin said, to which the elder nodded.

A few others had minor burns. There were two deaths among the young men who had so valiantly fought the dragon. Their fathers carried the bodies to the town square and laid them gently on the ground near Elder Andrew. His eyes clouded with tears and with one strong hand he gripped each man by the shoulder in turn.

"Brother William." Elder Andrew motioned toward Jasmine's father, who was already making his way to the center of the crowd.

"I can build their caskets in the morning," William said. "Might even have one the right size for Randall there." He motioned toward the smaller body. "You men can bring them to my workshop. I'll treat them respectfully, you know that. And we'll clean them up proper so you can say your farewells." His voice was soft, but it carried in the stillness of the night. The fathers nodded their wordless gratitude and once again lifted their sons to carry them to the woodworking shop.

"In the morning, those not dealing with our dead and wounded will gather here to assess the damage to our homes. We'll set up work details and try to get everyone patched up quickly. Does everyone have a place to sleep tonight?"

"My cottage was completely destroyed," cried Anna, the aging seamstress who lived on the edge of the village. "She hit me first."

"Anna can stay with us, Elder Andrew," called Clarissa. "We've extra room, and we weren't hit as badly." She hurried over to embrace Anna and escort her home to settle her in.

"We need to find out why the dragon attacked." Elder Andrew skewered them all with his stare. "Question your children, talk to your wives. We need to know if a nest has been discovered too close to the village. That's usually the reason. Someone may, God forbid, have broken our laws. We need to find the truth and deal with it. Now go home, get some rest. We have a lot of work to do."

Jasmine squirmed uncomfortably.

What does Elder Andrew know? He's old. I bet he never thinks about animals except to fill his belly with their meat. She sniffed. *Besides, my dragon will be different.* Her conscience smote her for her part in the night's tragedies, but she pushed those thoughts away. *No, this is for the good of the village. I'll show them. I'll show them all.*

~~~~~

For the next few days, it was harder and harder to break away. She couldn't thatch roofs or mend broken doors, or replace burned beams, but like most of the younger children in the village, Jasmine was sent back and forth between the well and the workers. She fetched water for them to drink and food from the tavern to keep them all sustained as they worked feverishly to mend every home in the village. Old Anna's house was a total loss, so for the moment, she would reside with the blacksmith and his wife. Once the repairs had been accomplished, they would all pitch in and build her another small cottage, perhaps more toward the center of the town, and thus, more protected.

The young boys in the village were put to the same tasks as the girls, carrying water and fetching tools, anything that needed to be done for the men. But Jasmine heard snatches of their conversations as they ran from one end of the village to the other.

"I'm going out to hunt for the nest," boasted Billy, the tanner's ten-year-old son.

"I'll come too," chimed Connor, the only son of the local herbalist, a widow.

"Better come armed with an axe," Billy said. "If we find the nest, we'll have to destroy the eggs."

"I just hope they haven't hatched already," said Henry, another of the village youth.
~~~~~

Elder Andrew heard the conversation too and stopped the boys. "You can go look for the nest, **if** your parents agree. But if you find eggshells only, you must come back and warn the village. Do **not** try to go after dragonets by yourselves. Do you understand me?"

"Yes, sir."

"Yes, Elder Andrew."

Jasmine tucked her head to hide the anger in her heart. *They are just going to kill the babies? What is wrong with these people?* She knew her thoughts were wrong, rebellious, and disrespectful of her elders. But why would they want to kill babies? She remembered Lightfire's beautiful golden eyes staring up at her so adoringly. Maybe she should try to find his siblings and guide them back to the grotto. But she knew that would be folly. Three more dragons would be too much for her to handle, but her heart ached for the poor, defenseless creatures.

As soon as she could, she slipped away to check on Lightfire. He crept into her lap as soon as she appeared in the grotto entrance, shivering a little as her tears fell on his scales.

"Oh, Lightfire!" she cried. "I wish I could save your brothers and sisters. But I can't. I know I can't. What are we going to do? I don't want them to find you. You're the only hope for our village. Why can't they see that? If we raise you and train you well, you'll be our greatest protection."

The little dragonet snuggled against her stomach and chirped softly.

"Jasmine! Where are you, girl?"

"Mother!" Jasmine cried. She lifted the dragonet back to his mossy bed and frantically grabbed some more berries to leave beside him. "I'll come back later. She can't find you now."

Jasmine raced to put as much distance between herself and the grotto as she could. If anyone found this place, Lightfire would never get the chance to prove his worth.

"We need every pair of hands to put our village back together, young lady," her mother stormed. "Why can't you listen when you're told to do something!" A stinging smack on her backside elicited a whimper from Jasmine as her mother dragged her back to the village.

"We found it! We found a nest!" Billy's voice brought the entire village to the clearing. People swarmed from their homes and businesses, as a small group of boys raced from the woods.

"Were there eggs?"

"How many eggs?"

"Where was it?"

The questions overlapped as the villagers surrounded the boys, who doubled over, hands on their knees as each lad fought to catch his breath.

Elder Andrew made his way to the center of the crowd and stood before the boys. "Did you find eggs?"

"No, sir," Billy said, gulping air. "Nothing but shells."

"And tracks," added Johnny, the son of the miller.

"Tracks?" murmured voices in the crowd.

"Big ones, headed for the mountains," said Billy. "But it seemed like something big went back and forth several times from the nest up the trail. Then the tracks would vanish. How could something that big just vanish?"

"She took her babes to the mountain before she attacked the village," said a deep bass voice. Jackson was a local hunter and trapper. He knew everything about every animal living. They all stood back respectfully as Jackson stood beside Elder Andrew. "And she didn't vanish, boy. She walked through the deepest woods, then flew as soon as she had room to spread her wings."

"But dragons have no fear of men," Elder Andrew protested. "Why would she think she wouldn't be returning to them?"

"Maybe something — or someone — had already raided her nest," Jackson replied. "In that case, she'd want to relocate the remaining dragonets to a more protected place."

Murmurs rippled through the crowd, and Jasmine's blood froze in her veins. *How could he know that?*

"Don't worry, Elder Andrew," Jackson said. "I'll do my best to track the dragonets down. If they're up on the mountain, though…"

Elder Andrew interrupted. "If they're up on the mountain, we leave them in peace. And we pray that they don't return to our woods again."

Jackson nodded and pulled Billy aside to question him more thoroughly about exactly where they found the nest.

Elder Andrew gave them a few moments, then called Billy back to his side. Gathering the boys together, he looked at them sternly. "What did I say to you boys about hunting the nest?"

"You said if our parents consented, and we asked. They said we could, Elder," said Johnny.

"And?" Elder Andrew prompted.

Silence.

Henry, the blacksmith's son, cleared his throat. "If we found a nest with shells, we were supposed to come back and tell you."

"And?"

Billy hung his head. "Do not go looking for the dragonets on our own," he said softly.

"That's exactly correct. So why did you disobey a direct order?"

Silence again.

"Sir, we weren't trying to disobey you, but we just wanted to be able to tell you which direction they went." Billy's voice trembled.

Elder Andrew sighed. "Boys, I know you meant well, but this could have ended very badly. Obedience is as important—no, maybe even more important—than bravery."

The boys hung their heads. Their fathers stepped forward and each took his son by the shoulders.

"Your orders, Elder Andrew?" the blacksmith asked.

Elder Andrew sighed. "I know your boys provide meat for your tables by hunting rabbits and squirrels in the woods, but…"

"We'll abide by your decision, sir," said the miller.

"No hunting for a month. No going into the woods for any reason. Extra chores in your places of business, and no leaving the village limits for any reason for that time period."

The men looked at one another and nodded simultaneously.

"No hunting at all?" Henry's voice squeaked slightly.

"Maybe a month of vegetables and bread will teach you a better lesson than I think up," said the blacksmith. "And since our entire family will suffer the same meatless fate, maybe next time you'll think about the consequences of your disobedience to the elder's orders."

The boys shrank. This was not the hero's welcome they had expected.

"Our rules are for the good of the community," Elder Andrew said gently. "If you do not learn this truth in the smaller things, what will happen when bigger issues are at stake? And even this could have ended so much more tragically if you had actually run into the dragonets. They are appealing as babes. You might have been tempted to rescue them, protect them. That would put the village at risk. If they were bigger than expected, we might not have found enough of your bodies to bury. How would your families feel then?"

Jasmine listened to the proceedings with growing distress. What punishment would Elder Andrew mete out if he knew that she'd stolen one of those eggs and that she was indeed protecting the dragonet in direct violation of the law? She hung her head to hide her shame, but it quickly melted into anger. She would show them just how wrong they were. She would prove that her dragon was going to change the rules.

~~~~~

Jackson returned the next day. He reported that he had scouted the entire area from the nest to the foothills of the mountain. From the looks of the nest, he estimated that three dragonets had hatched.

Murmurs swept through the crowd. Three? What if they all attacked at once? One dragon was an epic disaster, but three could mean the complete destruction of their village.

"I'll make a pass over the area over the next couple of months. By then, the dragonets will have grown enough that I might be able to catch a glimpse of them. If they stay on the mountain, we'll leave them alone. But if they venture down..." Jackson hesitated. "Well, we'll do what has to be done."

Jasmine's fists clenched at her sides. *Not if my dragon beats you to it*, she thought.

~~~~~

Jasmine stayed in the forest longer and longer each day, for her dragon was growing rapidly and seemed to require more and more attention. At first, Lightfire greeted her with curious cheeps and tilted his little head from side to side when she talked to him. After a few more berries and a bowl of water, he would curl up in her lap and sleep before awakening hungry again. Jasmine smiled as she stroked the animal's small head, for it was working as she had planned. The creature loved her and someday he would protect her village. She began bringing any scraps she could salvage from their dinner the night before.

As Lightfire grew, his appetite went beyond berries and table scraps. One morning, Jasmine returned to the grotto to find the desiccated remains of two small squirrels.

"Oh, no!" she cried. But when she tried to remove the carcasses, Lightfire screeched furiously and snatched them from her hands. He swallowed them, bones and all, in two gulps. Jasmine shook her finger and scolded the little dragon. "No, you mustn't..." She stopped. Her own family lived on meat. Who was she to tell a dragon he could not hunt?

"Oh, very well," she said with a sigh. "If you must eat meat, at least you don't expect me to catch it for you."

She sighed and pasted a smile on her chubby little face. "It's all right, Lightfire. I'm sorry I scolded you." She petted his head and he nuzzled her hand. "Guess I sounded just like my mother, didn't I?" she said. "We wouldn't want that."

As she ran her hand down the back of his head, she realized that his scales were hardening, and his spikes were no longer soft as goose down. Still, he seemed tame, and she knew she'd done right in claiming him for her own. He was the future protection of her village. Maybe Fall Feast would be a good time to bring Lightfire into the village. By then, he'd be big enough to be impressive, and she'd have him trained to protect them. If his siblings did come down from the mountains, they'd be in for a surprise!

~~~~~

A few weeks later, she returned to the woods to find the trees around her grotto blackened and the smell of burnt wood subtly blended with the wild herbs and the sunlit stream. A tremor tickled her stomach, but Lightfire seemed happy to see her, as he always was. He was the size of a large dog now, but he still tried to cuddle up on her lap. This time, a small puff of smoke from his snout scorched her skirt.

"Oh dear," said Jasmine. "How am I going to explain this burn mark to my mother?"

Lightfire looked up at her with curious golden eyes. They walked to the stream together and Jasmine tried to wash out the stain. It wouldn't wash away, but they played and splashed in the water until Jasmine forgot all about the small brown mark. Her distress over the blackened grotto was forgotten too, and she frolicked with her dragon in the sunlit woods.

~~~~~

"What have you done to your gown?" her mother asked with an exasperated sigh.

Jasmine's face blushed to the roots of her hair. "It's j-j-just mud, Mama," she stammered.

"You are worse than ten sons, Jasmine!" Her mother thrust her second dress at her. "Change into this and I'll scrub it this afternoon."

"But that one is too small," whined Jasmine, not wanting to give her mother the chance to examine her dress too closely.

"Well, that's too bad," said her mother angrily. "You shouldn't have been rolling in the mud. Take it off!"

Jasmine sighed and did as she was told, her mind running through a series of lies that might be believable. It seemed she'd done more and more lying since the dragon had come into her life. But it would be worth it one day. When she could bring Lightfire into the village and prove that he would be gentle with them, she would be vindicated. The deception would be worth it.

She tugged her gown over her head and took the old one from her mother's outstretched hand. As she wriggled into the dark green dress, she heard her mother gasp.

"Jasmine, this is not mud." Her mother's voice was softer than usual, but her tone was deadly serious. "This is a scorch mark. Have you been setting fires in the woods?"

"No, Mama," said Jasmine. At least in this matter, she could be truthful.

Her mother watched her closely, looking for signs of deceit as she continued. But this wasn't her usual scolding. There was a small thread of fear in her voice.

"Your father says you like to rescue animals, Jasmine, but… well… you… haven't rescued any… dragons … lately. Have you?"

"No, Mama," replied Jasmine in a small voice. Well, it was sort of true. She had indeed stolen a dragon egg, but it hadn't exactly been a rescue.

"Jasmine." Her mother spoke hesitantly this time. "Dragons look cute when they're young. But there is no beast quite like them. They are not tamable. They might act like you are their friend. But dragons are deceitful creatures, and they will turn on you sooner or later."

Jasmine said nothing, but her eyes glared at her mother. Lightfire loved her. He would never turn on her. Mama was wrong this time, and Jasmine was going to prove it.

"You do understand what I'm saying, don't you?"

"Yes, Mama," she said with ill-concealed anger. "I understand."

~~~~~

Each day, Jasmine was more and more convinced that Lightfire would be her village's defender. Soon she would take him before the Council and show them now tame her dragon truly was. Lightfire was the size of a great stallion now and endowed with a powerful
~~~~~

appetite. She rarely went into the grotto anymore; it was filled with the bones of more and more animals, and the stench was nauseating.

Instead, they played in the woods and splashed in the stream. Lightfire was learning to fly now, and Jasmine loved to ride on his back as he glided through the trees.

She still did not allow him to fly above the tree line for fear that he would be seen and shot down. But Jasmine loved to feel the wind whipping through her hair, enjoyed the exhilaration of soaring even if it was only a scant six or seven feet from the ground. Soon she would ride Lightfire right into the village square.

Then they would know she had done the right thing.

Still, the smell in the grotto bothered her, and she wondered what she could do to change the eating habits of her dragon.

~~~~~

Jackson came into the village the next day. His clothes were singed, and his face and hands bore heat blisters and burns. He sank beside the well, and Elder Andrew drew up a bucket of water for him. He drank greedily from the tin cup the elder pressed into his hands.

Elder Andrew grabbed Henry by the shoulder. "Fetch Fiona. Quickly, Henry. Tell her to come with her burn ointments. Run!" Then he turned back to the man. "Tell us what you can, Jackson," he said quietly. "Take your time."

Jackson took another cup of water from the elder and tried to clear his throat, but his voice came out raspy. Word had spread rapidly, and the village had gathered, waiting to hear his tale.

"I saw them yesterday. Up on the side of the mountain. They're about the size of full-grown horses now. Easier to spot. Two are green of body and their spikes are reddish colored. The third one is black with a silver breast. It was the most aggressive of the three. I didn't approach the mountain, but stood still and just watched to see what they would do."

Jackson's voice gave out, and he coughed violently, the spasms of it shaking his frame. He leaned back against the well as the elder gave him another cup of water. Fiona knelt beside him and tsked at the condition of his hands.

"Jasmine, come here, girl," she called as soon as she saw the child on the edge of the crowd.

Jasmine jumped, startled to be singled out, but she reluctantly stepped toward the midwife.
~~~~~

"Run to my cottage, child," she said, gripping Jasmine's arm tightly. "On my worktable to the right of the door is a basket with strips of linen for binding wounds. Bring it to me. And be quick, girl! Hurry!"

Jasmine ran to do her bidding and returned quickly, hoping she wouldn't miss too much of Jackson's story. Dread filled her little heart. What had happened to the dragons?

She handed the basket to Fiona and received a tight smile and nod for her service, but she could see the angry burns along Jackson's forearms. Even as Fiona smeared her ointment gently on the blisters, they burst and wept clear pus, then blistered again. Jackson gritted his teeth against the pain as she worked her herbal magic into his skin. Then as she wrapped his arms, he found his voice again and continued his tale.

"As I watched, the black dragon roared at me," he rasped. "I backed up a few steps, not wanting to be seen as a challenge to him. But he took to the air and flew off the mountain right at me. He shot flames right in my face." Jackson stopped to catch his breath, cough a few more times, then take another drink of water. "I've never seen a dragon act like that before. I wasn't threatening him, I didn't approach his territory, I never set foot on the mountain at all, Elder, I swear it."

"I know, Jackson," Elder Andrew said softly. "I trust your word. Try to continue if you can."

"He just kept circling around, then diving at me, shooting flames at the trees around me. I was surrounded by fire. There was a … a … malevolence…" He shuddered. "I was a dead man, and I knew it." He sagged against the well, trying to recover his composure. "I found myself curled in a ball on the ground, just praying for it to all end quickly. I couldn't fight something that wouldn't face me head on. It just kept flying at me then circling in the sky, then diving at me again."

Elder Andrew nodded to William, who dropped the bucket into the well and hauled up fresh water. The elder filled the tin cup yet again, and helped Jackson to drink from it as Fiona finished bandaging his hands.

"Suddenly the dragon flew right into the midst of the flames with me. He just stood there, staring at me with these huge red eyes. It … it was like he relished my pain! I've never been that close to a live dragon before. Not one like this." Jackson shuddered. "I gripped my axe in both hands and found the strength from somewhere to leap up and sink it into the beast's neck. It roared in pain, then it fell right on top of me! I don't know how I managed to squeeze myself out from under that body. God must have had a hand in it, because I could not have done it on my own." He coughed again.

"The other dragons on the mountain, Jackson. What did they do?" Elder Andrew asked. His voice was gentle, but there was an urgency to the question.

"I got away from the fallen dragon, and I looked up at the mountain. They were both screaming at me, screeching and flapping their wings." He swallowed hard, took another sip of water. "But they didn't venture down the mountain. Indeed, they went farther up the mountain. I don't think they'll be back." He sagged against the well, exhaustion catching up to him.

Fiona gently cleaned the soot from his face and began to treat the blisters on his cheeks and forehead. Jackson broke down and wept, but the minute the salty tears hit the blisters, he cried out in pain and passed out cold.

"It's better this way," she murmured. "Best he doesn't have to feel the pain of this part." She smeared her ointment on his face in thick layers, then looked around at the men. "Pick him up and take him back to my cottage. I'll have to tend him for some time to keep these burns from infection." The men did as she bid them, and she gathered her supplies into the basket that Jasmine had brought her.

Jasmine watched as the crowd slowly dispersed. She looked up to see Elder Andrew watching her intently.

"What did you think of Jackson's tale, Jasmine?" Elder Andrew asked her, his shrewd eyes staring holes into her heart.

"I think… I think he was lucky to get away," she said.

"Dragons are dangerous creatures," the elder said, nodding at her. "You should never harbor a dragon."

"**That** dragon was dangerous," Jasmine said, her voice louder than she intended. "That doesn't mean that **all** dragons are dangerous. Some dragons might be good. If they were raised by someone who loved them, they might not turn mean. They might…" She broke off her tirade as she noted the elder's eyebrows rising.

"Is there something you wish to tell me, my child?" he asked, bending down to meet her eye to eye.

"No, Elder Andrew," she said, staring intently at the weeds around the base of the well.

"Are you sure, child?" His voice sounded gentle. But she knew she could not trust him with her secret. He would order Lightfire's death if she confided in him.

"I have to go now, Elder Andrew. My mother will expect me to do my chores." She kept her eyes on those weeds. If she looked up, he would see the anger in her eyes, the rebellion in her heart. She had to protect her dragon until she could train him enough to prove to everyone in the village that Lightfire was different.

"Very well." Elder Andrew watched Jasmine flee. He saw William exit Fiona's cottage after helping deliver the unconscious hunter to her care.

"William, a moment please."

He approached the elder. Andrew placed a hand on his shoulder and spoke urgently to him for several moments. Jasmine watched the encounter from the corner of their home. What was the old man saying to her father? She saw her father's face pale, then he nodded briefly. They parted ways, but anger filled Jasmine's heart. Was the elder turning her father against her too? Was that what they had whispered about? She raced for the woods. Her only solace was that soon, Lightfire would be ready to be presented to the village. If she could only hold out for a few more days. Fall Feast was approaching. It was the perfect time. Everyone would be celebrating, happy, and Lightfire would impress them all with his loving behavior.

~~~~~

William tried to talk to Jasmine after dinner that night, but he didn't get far. He talked haltingly about dragon eggs being dangerous things, especially for little girls. She hadn't seen one, had she?

"No, Papa," she whispered, staring at the floor. He tried to pull her into his lap, but she pulled away and pleaded a headache. "Could I please go to bed now?"

He could think of no way to break her silence. She had retreated into her own little shell. Finally, he granted her permission and she scurried up the ladder to her loft. But she knew her parents would be watching her every move. She'd have to be very careful until the Fall Feast.

~~~~~

The day before the Fall Feast, a yearly celebration after the crops had all been harvested, her mother had spent all day turning out the beautiful golden loaves of bread for which she was well known. With such an abundance, Jasmine decided her mother couldn't possibly miss two loaves. She wrapped them in her apron and scampered into the woods the moment her mother's back was turned. She wanted to be certain that Lightfire would like the bread, for she planned to ride him into tomorrow's feast day celebration! If he did indeed eat the bread, she could slip out with several more loaves in the morning. Better to bring a dragon with a full belly to the village than a hungry one!

Lightfire stood upright on his hind feet at a good eight feet high now. His green and brown scales rippled and glinted with sunlight, and his claws were over six inches long. He was a marvelous sight.

"I brought you a treat," Jasmine said, eyes shining with anticipation. "Mama's bread is the best in the village." She broke the first loaf in half and held it up. Lightfire gulped it from her fingers and chewed before swallowing it. He screeched in delight as she laughed and held up the second half.

"I knew it!" she crowed with joy. "I knew you'd love Mama's bread. Everyone does, you know." Lightfire downed the second half, and eyed the other loaf greedily.

She held out the second loaf to break it, but Lightfire dipped his head quickly and ripped the whole loaf from her hands with his teeth. Pain shot through Jasmine, and she stared at her dragon in shock. He sat back, with the loaf clutched in his claws. He munched slowly on the first big bite, his eyes flickering at a new sensation. He stopped and stared at his newly acquired treat, then plucked a red-stained slice of something pink from the loaf. He licked the fleshy tidbit, then gulped it down and roared with approval.

Jasmine's body shook as she looked down at her hands, now slick with blood. Her index and middle fingers on her right hand were gone, and the smell of her own blood caused her breakfast to heave to the back of her throat.

"Mama!" she screamed, as Lightfire swallowed the second finger, chewing with a connoisseur's appreciation. He eyed her with fresh interest, his golden eyes glowing. He slurped the blood from his sharp talons.

"Jasmine! Where are you?" She heard her mother's voice. "Did you take some of the bread? It's for today's feast, young lady—"

"Mama! Help me!" Jasmine shrieked as Lightfire uncoiled his long neck closer to her. She backed away, stumbled over a root and fell on her back. She wrapped her bloody hand in her apron and tried to scoot backwards, but pain shot up her arm.

"Jasmine!" Her mother's voice filled with panic. "Jasmine! William, come quickly! Something's wrong."

"Over there!" shouted another voice.

"That scream came from farther into the woods," cried another voice. Elder Andrew. Jasmine knew that voice as well as she knew her parents.

"No, not like this. You were supposed to protect us," she whimpered.

Never harbor a dragon, Elder Andrew had said. But she hadn't listened.

Jasmine's fear and horror mounted as she watched the great beast loom over her and lick his lips in anticipation.

~~~~~

"So, children, who can name the laws of our village?" the elder asked, smiling brightly.

"Share with those who are in need," piped up a chubby little boy with solemn eyes.

"Take care of one another and protect your neighbors," said a sassy little pixie with blonde braids. "That's the first one."

"Never thteal," lisped a five-year-old, ginger-haired lad.

"Very good," said the elder, smiling broadly. "What else?"

"Honor the elders and obey their directions," said a tall, lanky boy with a shock of light brown hair that flopped in his eyes.

"Elder's favorite," whispered one of the girls in the back. She blushed when the elder leveled a penetrating glare in her direction.

"And you, Aurora," the elder asked, arching her eyebrows sharply. "Can you name another of our laws? You seem to have so much to say."

Aurora blushed as red as her carrot-colored hair. "Never harbor a dragon's egg." Her chin rose in defiance.

"Of course." The elder nodded. "And why do we have that rule?"

"Because dragons are supposed to be so vicious. But what if they aren't? What if they're just raised to be?" Aurora was only six years old, and the elder recognized the touch of rebellion.

"When a dragon is born," the elder began, "they look adorable. They are fairly helpless and love to cuddle with anyone who comes close, be it human or dragon. But they don't stay small and cute. They grow, and their nature is to destroy anything or anyone who they
~~~~~

think will try to control them." The elder held up her mangled right hand, which was missing two fingers. "I tried to raise a dragonet. I named him Lightfire, and I tried to teach him as best I could. I was so sure that he would protect our village if I showed him enough love."

The older children had heard the story many times, but a few of the younger ones gasped and their eyes widened in alarm.

"Then one day, I offered my dragon some bread. In taking it from my hand, he took my fingers. And he enjoyed the taste of human flesh. As he was about to pin me to the ground, my mother flung herself over me, covering my body with her own. The dragon took it as a challenge, because, to him, she was taking away his dinner."

"Did he kill your mama?" asked one fair-haired boy, his voice an awed whisper.

"Yes, he did," the elder said. "She gave her life for me. But she wouldn't have been in that position if I had followed the rules." She allowed the silence for a few minutes. "Now. You all have chores to see to. Off you go."

She watched them scurry in all directions. Pain washed over her. There hadn't been much left of her mother by the time the men had caught up with their axes and swords. They had hacked at the dragon from all sides until he bellowed one last shriek and fell to the ground. Jasmine had been badly burned by dragon flame, as well as the damage to her mangled hand. It had taken almost a full year for her to recover. The elder came often to sit by her bedside and help tend to her emotional recovery. It was decided that she had been punished enough and the lesson had been learned. But she still remembered the overwhelming realization that her mother loved her enough to step between her and an angry dragon. Her father had been right all along. She was loved. But the knowledge came too late to show appreciation.

When Elder Andrew grew old and his eyesight began to fail, he approached Jasmine and asked her to become the first woman elder in the history of their village.

"The village will never accept me as elder," she had exclaimed. "I almost got everyone killed by stealing a dragon egg!"

"The village has already accepted you, Jasmine," the elder had said gently. "They believe you have wisdom, which you learned the hardest way of all."

Her husband, Henry, had clasped her shoulders as he stood behind her. "You can do this, my dear," he had whispered in her ear. "You'll be an excellent elder. A fair one too."

Jasmine's head had reeled for days, but Elder Andrew was correct—as he always was! The village had warmly accepted her appointment and celebrated at the ceremony that marked the transfer of the mantle to her thin shoulders.

Now Henry came up behind her and slipped strong arms around her waist. "Tough day?"

"Rehashing the dragon egg lessons," she said with a wobbly smile.

Henry nodded toward their youngest daughter, Aurora. "She's been heading out to the woods every day. Should I follow her?"

"No," Jasmine smiled. "I'll do it. Hopefully, I won't have to throw myself in front of a dragonet today."

"Don't do that, my dearest," he protested with a laugh. "She's probably nursing a fawn or a baby fox."

"Probably," Jasmine agreed. "But we need to do something to nip her nursing in the bud. Or at least provide options. Did you do as I asked?"

"Yes," Henry laughed, "but are you sure it's wise?"

"I wish my parents had thought of it when I was younger. Maybe…" she broke off as her voice cracked.

"No 'maybes', my dear," Henry whispered as he kissed her cheek. "You survived, and I'm grateful for that." He turned and headed back to the carpenter's shop. His brother had taken over their father's blacksmith shop, and he had apprenticed with his father-in-law many years ago. Now he ran the family carpenter business, while his wife oversaw the village. He too had learned his lesson in dealing with dragons.

Jasmine followed Aurora into the woods. Her feet followed the familiar path to the brook and the burned-out grotto deep beneath the thick trees. Aurora jerked in surprise when her mother appeared. The baby raccoon in her lap sat up and scolded Jasmine, tiny fingers waving wildly in the air. It shoved a berry into its tiny mouth and chittered again.

Jasmine sat on the ground beside Aurora and reached out to stroke the tiny masked creature on the head. He settled back down on Aurora's lap.

"How did you find me?" Aurora whispered.

"Believe it or not, my daughter," Jasmine said with a laugh, "I used to come here all the time when I was your age. I took care of birds, foxes, squirrels... any creature that was injured or abandoned."

Aurora's eyes widened. "Was that... before the dragon?"

"Oh, yes," Jasmine said. "I couldn't face coming back here after I lost my mother."

"But this isn't a dragon, Mama! And I don't want him to end up in someone's soup pot." Tears gathered in her eyes.

"Someday, you might be tempted by a dragon, though, and I don't want that heartbreak for you. Our laws are in place for a very good reason, as I learned the hard way." Jasmine kissed her daughter on the forehead. "You are so much like me, darling."

"But I don't want to stop tending the animals." Aurora's face scrunched in frustration.

"All right," Jasmine said, considering her little daughter seriously. "What if we had another option?"

"Like what?"

"I've spoken with some of the men in the village, and your father has been helping me." Jasmine smiled gently. "How about a pen near our house where you can take care of your animals? They would be off limits to anyone looking to hunt. Once they've grown or healed and you've released them back into the woods, they might be fair game again. But that's our way of life. We hunt for meat. And other animals hunt for food as well. But as long as they are in your pen, they won't be bothered by anyone else in the village."

"So when will this pen be built?" Aurora said sulkily. "Next year?"

Jasmine's smile widened. "It's already built."

Aurora's head shot up and her mouth became a round O.

"I'm serious," she said. "We've taken care of it. Your 'animal hospital' can open today."

"A hospital? What's that?" Aurora's face scrunched up in a frown.

"Remember when those Crusaders came through here a few years ago?" she asked, her smile bright. Aurora nodded. "That's where I got the idea. The Hospitallers who traveled with the knights belong to an order of monks who have preserved healing knowledge. They have created places called 'hospitals' where they care for their wounded and sick. Brother Thomas told me all about it. Many monasteries have hospitals as part of their service to God and to their brothers. They've even created such places in the Holy Land for those injured in battle who can't travel back to their homes. Your hospital will be for the animals."

Aurora mulled over the idea. A place of her own! A sanctuary for her animals to heal. It sounded too good to be true.

"But what about the villagers? Will they really leave my animals alone?"

"Yes," Jasmine said decisively. Then she whispered, "I'm the elder. I can make it so." They giggled together, as she pressed her lips to her daughter's hair. The little raccoon chittered in agitation.

"Really?" Aurora asked, hardly daring to believe it.

"Really and truly. But there is one rule that must be obeyed."

Aurora's face fell. *Here it comes…*

"No dragons," Jasmine said softly, touching her daughter's cheek with her mangled hand. "No dragons ever."

Aurora smiled through her tears. "No dragons, Mama."

Gathering the baby raccoon in her apron, Aurora walked happily back to the village with her mother to see her new animal pen. Her Hospital.

No Dragons Allowed.

End

SILENCE IS GOLD
By Michelle L. Levigne

A bedraggled hawk circled Fragmar's courtyard twenty-four times before she noticed it, casting a tiny, flickering shadow over the scroll she was painstakingly copying. The original was ready to disintegrate from repeated handling, and she found as she neared her three hundredth birthday that she preferred to read an important reference rather than search the archives of her brain and hope she recalled accurately. If she hadn't paused to consider the verb tense in the high scholarly language of Reshidor, she might have copied the wrong word, when the flicker of shadow changed one rune into another. Sighing, she considered living up to the cranky reputation of dragons everywhere and shooting a spout of flame at the winged interrupting messenger.

Any bird brave and strong enough to fly out here into the desert where she kept her scholarly retreat had to be there as a messenger. No bird was foolish enough to go to all that effort and interrupt her just to gossip. Except maybe crows. But they were arrogant troublemakers anyway.

"What do you want?" she rumbled. Two inner lids slid across her eyes as she tipped her head back to look up at the noonday sun and the tiny black fleck flying across it.

"Begging your pardon, Fragmar," the hawk rasped as it finally dropped from high enough to be just out of reach of her flame. "It's Elysto again."

"Of course." She sighed, a few smoke rings escaping her nostrils.

Fragmar almost forgot the rules of hospitality, but she refused to take out her irritation at being interrupted on the hawk. Elysto could talk the stars down out of the sky. And had, on at least three occasions she could remember. All of them disastrous. Why blame the hawk? He was only living up to the vows made to the Unseen, for all raptors to act as messengers in times of danger and need and disaster. If Elysto hadn't been born a warrior unicorn, massive and muscle-bound, terrifying with the sharpness of his horn and the flames he could shoot from horn and nostrils, he would have been a philosopher or diplomat. He loved to talk and lecture and cajole. He seemed to think he had been designated by the Unseen to solve the world's problems. He also seemed to think because Fragmar was one of the rare pink-and-lavender dragons and a scholar, that meant she was born to help him.

She disagreed, but Elysto rarely shut up long enough for her to tell him he was wrong. The best tactic when dealing with the big black unicorn was to let him speak his piece, give the assistance he demanded, and thank the Unseen when he went away again.

"If you don't mind cooked meat, or spices, there's a lovely muskox I prepared the other day. Plenty left." She gestured with a flick of her head on her long, serpentine neck, toward a shadowy corner of her courtyard. She had entertained herself many years ago turning the small room into an oven large enough for an elephant, and regularly experimented with baking and roasting to relax in between moon-long scholarly research sessions.

"I've heard that about you," the hawk responded with a raspy chuckle. "Why do you fiddle with this thing Humans call cooking?"

"All knowledge is useful, at one time or another. Besides, sometimes I have visits from nobles and scholars and the occasional warrior on a quest. It confuses them if I offer them cooked food, and that makes them much easier to deal with." She busied herself capping the massive inkwell and putting her ivory and gold pens into tall containers of water, to soak them clean. When Elysto called for her help, experience told her she wouldn't return to her scholarly pursuits for several days, or longer. "What sort of trouble did the old battlebrute get into this time?"

"Helping someone out of trouble, and he's in the middle of it, otherwise he'd have come himself," the hawk responded, his words muffled by a mouthful. "My word, this is lovely. I think I need to find someone with hands, to do some cooking for me and my flock."

Fragmar chuckled as she took the dried scroll and put it away for safekeeping. Fortunately, it never rained in the desert where she lived, so she didn't have to worry about the weather disturbing her piles and hills and mounds of books and scrolls and scholarly papers. She also didn't have to worry about anyone having the temerity, or foolishness, to try to break into her home while she was away.

Because of course, if Elysto was so overwhelmed with whatever trouble he had stuck his horn into now, she could be away for some time. If he weren't her closest friend, and if he didn't leave her alone for a decade at a time, she might have been annoyed. She was a dragon, after all. Dragons were supposed to be solitary. Why couldn't he let her be solitary?

"Now, what's the problem this time?" she said, settling down for a long talk, once the hawk had finished eating. He perched on a high mud-brick wall and preened his feathers for a few seconds, and she waited only slightly impatiently. There were social niceties to obey, after all.

Granted, social niceties and all that time wasted when she could be studying, was why she was grateful she was a dragon. Most creatures and Humans left her alone without asking why they should do so.

"Fidus," the hawk said, and now his bedraggled condition made perfect sense.

For decades, Elysto had brought her news of the creeping blight of Fidus, the Deceiver. He devoured kingdoms from within, withering them, draining all life, and moving on. Occasionally Fidus faced a hero who resisted him. Most heroes fell. They depended on strength of arms but neglected the strength and health of their souls. Occasionally, a teacher or a sage faced Fidus. They often fared better, but after a time, they also fell. He was the Deceiver, after all. When he could not overcome the champions of the Unseen, Fidus merely waited until they grew frail and died. The evil magic at his core granted him a type of immortality. He took over the bodies of the defeated, draining them of their years, their strength, their riches and power.

On a regular basis, Elysto badgered Fragmar until she joined him to lecture and advise the target kings, their nobles and advisors. She quoted from hundreds of years of wisdom and cited examples. Those who warded Fidus from their borders in the power of the Unseen. Those who fought in their own power and failed. Occasionally, he let her write long letters with that information, instead of making her join him to face down the stubborn and foolish. Fragmar hated to admit it, but words of warning coming from a dragon, even a pink-and-lavender one, sometimes had more impact than if they came from a fire-breathing, horn-waving, furious black unicorn. Unfortunately, when Elysto needed Fragmar to join him and intimidate with her size and flames, the situation was usually too far gone to remedy.

She thanked the Unseen that Elysto had sent a messenger, instead of coming to her himself. Chances were good she didn't need to leave her fortress this time. And maybe there was hope for whatever kingdom he tried to save. More important, he would leave her alone in blissful, scholarly silence for another decade.

"How bad is it?" Fragmar asked the hawk.

"Elysto thinks he caught it in time."

"Define 'in time' please?" She sighed, trying to be grateful. She could almost recite the words with the hawk, because she had heard them many times over the decades.

"The diplomats are still preening and pretending to be friendly. Elysto wants you to work your usual magic with letters and documents full of history and persuasion."

"Yes, he would." She sighed again, producing thicker smoke rings. It was her own fault. Elysto knew just how to flatter her, calling upon her love of scholarship to contribute in his never-ending quest to save the world and cure its ills.

No one would be able to cure the soul-deep ills of the world until the Unseen fulfilled prophecy and brought about the Restorer. She supposed she admired Elysto for trying, despite the constant failures.

She doubted her work this time would be any more effective than the last dozen times. Humans had a nasty tendency to believe, even if unconsciously, that they would be the exception to history. Even when history proved them wrong.

That was one of Fidus' nastier and most effective tricks.

"Tell me everything you know," Fragmar said. "There are more hawks coming to carry everything I write, aren't there?"

The hawk chuckled and bobbed his head, and they settled down for a long talk. The names of the countries and kings involved, the inroads Fidus had already made, the diplomats who had been duped or coerced or enchanted into supporting Fidus. They talked for three hours, while she made a long list of notes. When the hawk flew away, she got to work, ransacking the many long hallways and rooms lined with books and scrolls and tablets, and the massive chests filled with meticulously filed notes she had made in her centuries of study. Fragmar searched for three days for all the references she needed. She outlined for one day, wrote for the next three. The hawk returned with seven others, and even then they nearly weren't enough to carry the four scrolls and five thick, loosely bound volumes of notes and letters. Fortunately, Elysto had plenty of experience with her scholarship and thoroughness, and had worked with several Human allies to fashion slings to hold all her work safely, while the hawks flew in pairs.

Fragmar sighed as the results of her work vanished against the sunrise. She crooned a prayer to the Unseen to keep the hawks safe in their long flight. She asked for success in Elysto's mission to talk some sense into the kings now being threatened by Fidus' false friendship and promises of wealth and power and safety. His words were as much poison to the souls and hearts of Humans as the desiccating, draining magic that turned their kingdoms into wastelands.

Then, trying to convince herself she had done as much as she was able, using the talents the Unseen had given her, she settled down with a satisfied sigh and returned to her project. That scroll wouldn't last much longer, and it was one of her favorites because the prophecies contained in it were so convoluted and obtuse. She quite hoped she would live long enough to see them all fulfilled.

Fragmar was a dragon, after all, and as well as being long-lived, that meant a solitary life. She was grateful the Unseen had made her that way. All the qualities of dragonhood suited her temperament.

All dragons hoarded. What the world didn't seem to understand was that many dragons valued other things than gold. Some hoarded uncut gemstones. Others hoarded fine weaving. Some traveled the world, capturing music to magically embed in instruments that played themselves.

Fragmar hoarded silence. Her solitude was a vital weapon to protect her silence.

The world at large thought she lived in Spearpoint Summit, but the warren of tunnels and caves was only for show, a distraction. She visited the cave perhaps once every other moon, to respond to messages from fellow scholars and take deliveries of books from merchants, whom she paid very well. She put up walls of old, useless books no one read anymore, creating a labyrinth to confuse and intimidate any fool who ignored the warning signs and the spells that demanded they stop in the first cave and speak their business. In truth, Fragmar resented the paper, leather, parchment, and ink wasted on the writings of self-appointed prophets and wise men. She collected their books first to stop the spread of their delusions of misguided wisdom, and then to use them as walls. The books she valued were kept in her fortress in the desert. After all, caves were damp. She had better things to do with her magic than expend it constantly warding off mold. The books seen by the occasional, unwelcome visitors were dipped in lacquer to seal and preserve them. All the better to keep fools from opening the books and being tainted by the foolishness within them.

"Not that any fool has ever managed to steal a book from me," she had confided once to Elysto when he had come in person to visit her, and brought her several valuable scrolls.

"They don't try to steal the books *because* they're fools," he had said, snorting sparks from his nostrils and hollow, spiral horn.

Now, Fragmar sighed and welcomed the growing heat as the dawn turned to full day. She did love the heat. That was why she had built her home in a rambling fortress at the core of a desert that stretched a hard ten days' ride in all directions. The dry heat preserved her precious books. Nothing made her happier than to curl up in her open courtyard with a pile of books and scrolls, enact a light spell, and read without interruption for a moon at a time. Which she intended to do once she had finished copying that very valuable scroll.

Dragons didn't need to eat or sleep very often. Fragmar could go a day at a time without moving anything more than the taloned foot that picked up and opened and closed books and turned pages. Such was her bliss. Perhaps every three days she turned and drank from the deep well supplied by the water tables she had diverted all across the desert. She wished she had some other source of water, sometimes. Diverting all the water tables had formed a tunnel, an underground pathway to her fortress. It was a weakness she couldn't combat, because water was necessary for life. Elysto used the tunnel when he came to visit her.

If she was lucky, he would be busy with his newest save-the-world project for a decade, maybe more. Fragmar settled down to read and copy and study, and prayed that Fidus' evil would finally turn on him and devour him. Then she could be assured of peace, at long last.

~~~~~

Elysto came charging up the underground stream that sparkled with phosphorescent fish and water weeds. Fragmar buried her head under a pile of books. She whimpered and silently pleaded with the Unseen that this was just a bad dream. Why couldn't he content himself with sending messengers for more letters? She knew she was
~~~~~

being selfish to complain, because he had left her alone for nearly twenty years. Why hadn't he learned that all his efforts to save the world were useless?

Humans were foolish, frail creatures and yet amazingly resilient. There were always remnants who clung to the land Fidus devastated, who fought hard and brought back life decades after he had abandoned their lands like rubbish. How many kingdoms were flourishing now that had once been wastelands? Why keep interrupting her to try again, when they both knew it was useless?

"Fidus is making overtures to Vivian and Cornagar," Elysto announced, as he appeared from the mouth of the tunnel, at the far end of her courtyard.

Fragmar flinched and a dozen or so books fell off the pile hiding her head.

Vivian and Cornagar, the Green Lady and the Horned King, weren't like other Human rulers. They were guardians of the Heartwood, the deepest, oldest forest of all, the place where the Unseen had brought forth life. The Unseen had promised someday, He would walk again through the Heartwood and set all things right.

"They have too much common sense to listen to Fidus." Fragmar's words were muffled even in her own ears, under all those books.

A sharp, hot stab in the tip of her long tail startled her. Elysto's mistake was in staying there after he poked her. Did the old fool think she wouldn't retaliate? Fine, then he had to learn his lesson all over again!

Fragmar whipped up her tail, smacking him hard enough to send him stumbling away a dozen clattering steps. He knocked over a stack of clay tablets. Some shattered as they hit the packed dirt of her courtyard. Sighing, she pulled her head out of the pile of books.

For such a small creature, in comparison to her vast armor-plated bulk, Elysto had an incredible talent for stubbornness and resilience. He was taller than the tallest man she had ever seen, but she could have stepped on him. Granted, at risk of getting that horn shoved through her foot, and probably poisoned. Unicorns were able to heal by pulling poison and sickness out of the dying. What the world at large didn't know was that unicorns could store all the sicknesses and poisons they removed. At need, or just in a fit of temper, they then inflicted that noxious, acid substance on those foolish enough to attack or try to capture them. Even if he did consider himself her best friend, that was no guarantee Elysto wouldn't give her a hot foot that would ignite her interior fires for the first time in decades.

Why she loved and admired the interfering, stubborn, argument-waiting-to-happen who insisted on trying to save the world, she had no idea.

"They have to let him into the Heartwood to hear him," Fragmar said, coiling up her tail to keep it out of his reach. "They won't."

"Not at first, anyway. His dupes believe the stories they tell, so their sincerity covers over the lies. How long do you think Vivian and Cornagar will be able to stand up against rational, pleasant people who tell them the honorable thing to do is at least listen?"

"I'm a witness," she said. "I know just how persuasive the words 'what harm would it do?' can be."

Elysto snorted and stomped his silver hooves, scattering sparks and blowing puffs of steamy flames. Fragmar extended her tail as a barrier between his angry huffs and the closest books. The old grump didn't even have the grace to look a little ashamed, but he clearly knew she was talking about him.

"No more warning and advising. This time, we need to strike first," he said, and shook his head so his mane snapped hard against his ebony flanks.

"Your grandfather tried that. He found out it isn't so easy to skewer Fidus through the heart when there is no heart."

"If the Heartwood falls --"

"It will not fall. The Unseen promised that."

"The Unseen promised many things. We don't understand most of them until long after the prophecy has come true." He stomped his forefeet, making the sand rumble and dance, until the grainy dust rose and clung to his sweat-soaked beard and dulled the gleaming silver of his fangs. "We must act, Fragmar, before it is too late."

There were so many ways she could have responded to that. All Fragmar cared about was getting Elysto to go away again. She admitted she had grown jaded. Or was the correct word "cynical"? She just couldn't see the point in abandoning her cozy oasis and the accumulated knowledge of centuries. For what? Flying out, breathing fire, sharpening her talons to attack an enemy who could not be defeated by force? Fidus the Deceiver did not triumph through force. He slithered and crept and soaked into the mind and soul and heart. He weakened the will and confused the mind, and as he had no body of his own, he could not be killed.

Death for him wouldn't "take," and become permanent, as far as anyone knew. There were many thousands of books in the world Fragmar either had not obtained or hadn't read yet. She needed her solitude and her silence to continue her studies, and someday find the answer to that vexing problem. What would at long last kill Fidus?

"I have learned a few things about Fidus that I can put into another letter."

"One of these days, you'll need to do more than write letters," Elysto growled.

"Anyone who won't listen to the advice of a dragon is already lost and defeated. Vivian and Cornagar aren't fools."

She wrote the letter, and rewrote it four times, to make sure it spelled out clearly the concerns from centuries of watching Fidus devour the nations of the world. At long last, Elysto trotted away down the underground tunnel, not quite satisfied, not quite placated. Silence returned to her fortress.

A moon-cycle passed, and Elysto didn't return with any news. She knew he would only bring her bad news. If Fidus were defeated by the Green Lady and the Horned King resisting him, then the entire world would be shaken and the stars would dance in the sky, and she would know healing had come.

Fragmar discovered she was wrong about the reaction to the battle between the rulers of Heartwood and Fidus.

The silence from Elysto stretched out over many moons, which turned into years. At the end of three years, Fragmar changed the message in the spell at the entrance cave of Spearpoint Summit, asking for news of the Green Lady, the Horned King, and Heartwood. The few merchants who regularly searched the world for the books she valued often took a year or two between visits, so she didn't expect a response for some time. However, now no foolish adventurers approached the cave, seeking treasure or to prove their prowess in battling the dragon of the mountain, or seeking answers to riddles plaguing other lands and far-off kingdoms. Fragmar didn't find that sudden change in irritating traffic worrying until two more years had passed.

The first response to her request for news of Heartwood didn't come from scholarly friends on the other side of the world. She had hoped for something by now, even if just to say they had heard nothing bad. The long silence threatened to cool her interior fires. Were the other scholars too busy dealing with problems and threats in their own lands? Or were they in hiding?

When Humans truly believed magical places and people existed, they wanted to confront them and profit from them, and eventually control and remake and destroy them. Magical creatures like Elysto and Fragmar had learned long ago to be fearsome and rare and solitary, if they wanted to survive. Fear held back envy, but even that only worked for a short time. Wonder was no protection.

The response to her request came in the shape of several books. Most of them badly made, full of smeared ink and fables, to entertain nobility and frighten the new generation into obedience and common sense. Each of the books labeled the existence of the Green Lady, the Horned King, and Heartwood as nothing but fables.

That was comforting. As long as Humans doubted the existence of the Heartwood and its rulers, they wouldn't threaten it. They would feel foolish going on quests to find and conquer it, and would mock anyone who proposed or tried such a thing. Doubt was a powerful defense for the magical.

The day the writers of such books started to say things such as, "They once existed," and even reported on the people who had found and entered Heartwood, Fragmar would fear. Because by then it would be too late. What Humans believed in, they wanted to control, after all. Too many self-appointed wise men and historians only admitted something had become a legend after it had been eradicated or changed until it was unrecognizable.

She shivered a little and contemplated taking a long journey to seek some of her scholarly friends whom she only knew through correspondence that sometimes took a year between letters. The thought of leaving her dry, hot fortress and abandoning her books to the depredations of sandstorms made her feel somewhat ill. Some of that illness came from shame.

She wrote letters and took long, moonlit flights to Spearpoint Summit to drop them off, for merchants to take and begin the long process of delivery. There were dozens of reasons why her friends hadn't responded yet, starting with bandit attacks on land and sea destroying letters. Common sense said to wait, to sit still, and take comfort that Elysto hadn't come charging up the water tunnel, demanding her help. That had to be a good sign, didn't it?

Fragmar believed so, until she looked up from several days of studying and went to take a long drink.

The water tasted bitter.

She spat it out, put her head in deeper and drank from the bottom of the well.

Her head touched bottom far sooner than it should have. Logic said the flow of water from the desert water tables had slowed. Perhaps some tables had dried up?

She sat back to calculate the passage of time. How long since Elysto came to pester her? Fragmar raised her head to the night sky and studied the stars for the first time in … how long? She found the time-charting stars and measured how much they had moved since the last time she studied the sky. Twelve years? How could Elysto have been so busy he hadn't come to chat, to scold her for her solitary life, and demand she do something about the fate of the world?

Maybe … maybe silence wasn't a good sign after all?

Fragmar studied the water tables of the desert. She identified the specific source of the bitter water. A shudder ran through her when she determined it came from the mountain-girdled valley that held Heartwood.

She left at sunset and flew, skimming low to the ground, seeking for signs of Elysto.

He found her before she found him. After all, a pink-and-lavender dragon more than 100 cubits long was easy to spot in the sky. Especially when the trees of Thunderfalls Pass, that once reached up high to tickle her belly … no longer existed.

Fragmar landed quickly, confused by the thick clouds that hung low to the ground, and then by the changed landscape below the rolling blackness. She stumbled through the marshy plain where there was once a rolling green meadow thick with healing herbs. She struggled for breath and trembled, hating the taste of sickness in the air, oozing upward from the ground. If any herbs remained, they no longer healed. Everything was rot and encroaching death.

Elysto leaped at her, trumpeting fury. He shook and foamed at the mouth and stomped and snorted until flames came out of his nose and his horn and his fangs dripped luminous purple venom.

"What took you so all-fired long?" he demanded, when he finally got his breath and his temper under control again.

Fragmar shook her head. Had he said other things and she hadn't heard?

"I … never got your message?" she finally said.

"What message?" Another stomp, and the sparks from his silver hooves dried up some of the marshy, soggy ground around them.

The smell from the baked ooze was no better than the raw, wet ooze.

"Why did you expect me to come if you didn't send me a message?"

"You honestly don't pay attention to what's going on out here, do you? You finally put up the wall you've been threatening me with, didn't you?"

"No. You know me, Elysto. I get into a scholarly puzzle and I don't look up for moons at a time."

"Yes." He blew a great gust of flame and smoke. "Heartwood has fallen."

"How?" Fragmar braced to hear him blame her.

"How does it always happen? They listen to our warnings, then after a while they think they're safe and they relax and make mistakes, or they think they're smarter than us and they decide to do things their own way."

"And they listen to the Deceiver." One huge tear escaped her left eye, steaming as it slid down her lavender scales, before hitting the ground. Elysto snorted and jumped back so he didn't get splashed.

"Sometimes I think you're right. Let them stumble and fall and learn their lessons the hard way. Maybe they'll learn faster if we don't help them." He sighed and slowly lowered himself to the ground, to curl up next to her right foreleg. He looked tiny and frail next to her, delicate, despite his muscles and horn and fangs and the sharp edges of his hooves, and the scorpion sting on the end of his whiplash tail.

"Are they dead, or are they slaves?" she asked, after the quiet of the ravaged landscape settled into a soft throbbing around them. Like the deep breathing of a child who cried herself to sleep.

"Worse." He made a rumbling sound like he would either growl or pass wind. "Fidus worked through some obsequious flatterer named Hafbaek, who got thrown out of his own kingdom. He got *between* Vivian and Cornagar. Convinced them the other was plotting with Fidus. They're separated. That's how Fidus got in. Right now, all his slaves are building a castle for Hafbaek, to hold the land for him. Chopping down all the trees of Heartwood that resist them. Any that are sickly and falling asleep, they leave standing." He shuddered and pulled himself to his feet. "The worst part is, the castle *encloses* the core of Heartwood. The enemy can't get to the tree throne, but they've made sure nothing can get out, and no one else can get in to mend things. Vivian and Cornagar are too busy blaming each other. Eventually, they'll calm down and when their wounds stop screaming at them, they'll start thinking again. They'll come together and work together. Fidus is making sure when that happens, they can't get to the tree. If he hasn't killed it by then."

"Could we get to the tree?" Fragmar held her breath again.

Elysto backed up a few steps and tipped his head back and looked into her eyes. "How?"

She spread her wings, knocking over trees in the process. He grinned, baring his fangs, and sparks filled his eyes.

The plan was simple. Fragmar clutched Elysto carefully, but tightly, against her chest. His legs hung down, and he kept his head bowed so his horn didn't poke her. It wasn't dignified, but neither of them cared about dignity.

Her wings ached by the time they reached the place where Heartwood once stood. The ache and exhaustion were stronger in her soul than in her body. She wept steaming tears to see the destruction. Trees from the dawning of time had been cleared away, a scar slashed by a broken knife. Fragmar couldn't see the core of Heartwood and the tree throne where Vivian and Cornagar had served the Unseen, dispensing healing and justice and knowledge. A black, churning haze covered the forest, marking the place where the axes stopped and the stonemasons struggled to build the wall of the castle.

No one looked up, no one reacted as they flew overhead. Fragmar's huge shadow faded into the general gloom covering the denuded landscape. It thickened with every beat of her massive wings. The air was cold, with a sting like acid. Rotting green streaks shot through the haze and gathered into a churning knot right over the spot where she imagined the tree throne still sat in defiance.

The only question was if the tree throne generated that dark haze, the sickly streaks of energy, to keep the enemy out, or if the haze was part of its prison.

"Ready?" Elysto shouted, and kicked his legs a little.

"I don't know if this is wise."

"Too late now!" His kicking became a running motion. He bowed his head, pointing his horn at the center of that churning.

Fragmar swooped down, to get closer to the haze, to the open circle of land around the tree throne. This was the tricky part. She had to extend her legs, holding Elysto as far away as she could, swing him back and forth a few times to build up momentum, and then throw him down, without being able to see where he would land.

The haze churned. Fragmar let Elysto slide down. She gripped his chest with her forepaws, and her hind paws gripped where his hind legs joined his torso. She swung him back. He let out a yelp she hoped was glee and excitement, and not cussing terror. A frightened unicorn was not safe to be around. One who could cuss a poisonous green streak, like Elysto, was even more dangerous.

Forward, then another swing back.

"Now!" he shouted.

She flung him forward and out in as graceful and powerful an arch as she could.

The churning below turned into a geyser of blackness streaked with sickly green-gray-red, like a rotting wound. Black lightning slashed upward and curled claws around Elysto. It swirled him around three times and flung him hard and fast, so he vanished from sight, cussing and howling.

The black lightning slapped at her. She tumbled head over heels across the sky. Icy wind enfolded her and the tops of mountains tried to rip her wings off her back. She landed hard, so the ground broke underneath her and she tunneled down through granite as if it were sand caught in a churning tide. Her interior fire went out completely.

~~~~~

When Fragmar's fire relit, she needed to dig out of the hole that had collapsed around her. Grass and bushes and trees had grown up over the scar of her passage through the ground. She had a hard time focusing her eyes at first, to study the stars and determine how long she had slept.

Thirty years, give or take. She just wasn't up to being picky about the degrees of difference in the dance of the stars. Fragmar's wings were stiff with abuse and disuse, so she walked out of the distant forest and the crumbling foothills. She walked for a moon before she was up to flying again, and then flew the rest of the way to her desert fortress.

While she slept, the disintegration of the Heartwood had affected other lands around it. The desert's water tables had been altered, along with the migration paths of animals and merchants. The watered lands encroached on Fragmar's desert, but she still had a decent border of intimidating sand and heat around her fortress.
~~~~~

She spent a year putting things to rights, and found a few brave souls among the merchant caravans passing by, who didn't flee in jibbering terror when a voice spoke out of a dust storm, asking for news of the world. No merchants had come to her cave on Spearpoint Summit in all the time she had been gone, so she needed to find her sources of news and books elsewhere.

She found some encouragement that the world in general seemed to believe in magic and magical creatures again, and didn't immediately class them as monstrosities in opposition to the Unseen. Her magic had regenerated sufficiently to send gold and gemstones to an oasis two days of travel away from her fortress, and retrieve the books and letters left by the merchants.

The news of the world was not encouraging.

Hafbaek was now an elderly king with a handsome brute of a son. His castle was the wonder of the world, larger than a city, with an enchanted garden and captive sorcerers in the belly of the castle. There were no doors leading inward to the garden. Or so said those brave enough to risk the mighty king's wrath to explore and spy where they weren't welcome.

The Green Lady and the Horned King were the source of many legends now, and few of them even hinted at the truth of Heartwood. Tales spoke of a great stag who spoke with the voice of a man and roamed the vast, sprawling, deadly dark forest that encroached on Hafbaek's kingdom. That was the one thing the usurper king feared. None of his warriors or servants who went into that forest ever returned. Other rumors spoke of a man who had gathered a band of bandits around himself. He rarely spoke with words, and when he fought, he roared like a furious stag. He never rode but went on foot, faster than any horse could run. Other rumors spoke of a silent woman with green hair, who roamed the highways leading into Hafbaek's kingdom. Her hair moved like creatures from the depths of the sea. Anyone who saw the green-haired woman and retained his sanity counted himself lucky. Her hair could pull men from their saddles and strangle horses. It twined itself around wagons and carriages and chariots, and then pulled them apart like a man would rip parchment with his hands.

Of Elysto, the fire-breathing warrior unicorn, there was no word.

Fragmar settled down into her precious silence and her studies, and waited for Vivian or Cornagar to give up their violent response to the loss of Heartwood, and approach her for advice. Experience of centuries had taught her that offering advice in these situations never did any good. Those who had fallen from high positions and great responsibility needed to ask before they could be helped and healed.

Then there was that spectacular, embarrassing failure to get to the tree throne. She feared if they had heard, and hadn't learned humility in the last thirty years, that alone ensured they would never come to her for help.

She told herself that was fine. Dragon had never equated hero, no matter what land, no matter what legends, no matter how desperate the people were for someone to rescue them. Common sense said to run away from dragons when they appeared, not run to them.

So when an approaching girl set off the warning spells in the water tunnel, Fragmar was surprised enough to go investigate. Decades ago, her only visitors to come through the water tunnel, other than Elysto, were silly boys who had found a magical sword or an invulnerability ointment and wanted to make a name for themselves by fighting a fire-breathing dragon. They were offended to discover she was pink and lavender and had taken to enameling her talons. They either had temper tantrums or burst into tears of mortification when she picked them up by an ankle and flew them a moon's journey away from her fortress.

Trained warriors had far more intelligence than to pick a fight with a dragon who would share her wisdom if they asked politely. With so many tyrants and bandit lords ravaging the land and rebelling against overlords, warriors didn't have time to look for magical creatures to fight. Humans were monsters far more dangerous and numerous, and more profitable to fight, than anything hiding in mountain caves or dark forest glades or deep under the sea.

Fragmar came upon the girl in one of the lighted areas of the water tunnel, where a spire of stubborn rock thrust up through the sand overhead and allowed a chimney to form. The opening was too small at the top for more than a small bucket or a waterskin to fit through. Fragmar had amused herself over the years by decorating the chimneys up to the desert with polished metal to funnel light down to the tunnel. This encouraged all sorts of water-loving creatures to set up housekeeping, including frogs and diving birds.

Fragmar kept her tail curled up so it didn't drag, and made little noise as she went down the tunnel. She approached within a bowshot of the girl before the intruder noticed her. The girl was distracted, kneeling on the edge of the pool and studying the jeweled fish and multi-colored frogs swimming in the pure, sweet water. Fragmar was very proud of the little oases of color and life her engineering work had encouraged over the years. Even a dragon couldn't spend every minute of her life studying.

"You're a puzzle, now, aren't you?" Fragmar said, and settled down on a shelf of cool, damp rock, to stay out of the flow of water.

The girl was dressed like a woodland warrior, a mixture of leather and triple-thick homespun: tunic, vest, trousers, knee-high boots, with a traveler's bag slung from a long strap across her chest. She had no weapons, other than an eating knife at her waist, carried no shield, and didn't stink of fire-warding ointment. Fragmar couldn't calculate how many innocent salamanders had been sacrificed over the centuries to create an ointment that could barely withstand regular flames, forget about a dragon's rock-melting temperatures.

The girl raised her head and settled back on her haunches. Just for a moment, her face was in the shaft of light. Her eyes sparkled green like fresh leaves of basil and a few strands of green flickered in her hair, there and gone again like an illusion.

"Who are you?" Fragmar felt justifiably proud of herself that she didn't shout, didn't roar, and didn't whimper, especially.

"Ivy." She took a deep breath. "Vivian's daughter."

"Ah. That explains ... very little." She surprised herself by chuckling.

That seemed to surprise Ivy, too. She shifted backwards and her foot slid on the damp rock, so she nearly skidded down into the water.

"So why are you here? For advice? To demand assistance? Demand I fly you over the imprisoned forest so you can try to drop onto the tree and take it back by spilling your own blood all over it?"

"I have things I want to do, need to do before ... I'm going to try to break through the castle. But I wanted to make sure the legends were true, and ask you what really happened when my mother and the Horned King fell."

"You don't trust the story Vivian told you?" Fragmar didn't like that. She would have expected Vivian to tell the truth. No matter how badly she was deceived, no matter how much she might have argued with Cornagar and blamed him.

"My mother never told me. I was too young when she attempted the castle and never came back." Ivy shrugged. "The old grump throws so many lectures into the story, I can't follow it."

"The old grump?" The fires stirred inside her, more awake than they had been in years. "You don't mean Elysto survived?"

"He raised me, as much as he could. He would have kidnapped me and dragged me away from my father and our soldiers a dozen times, if he could have."

"You have soldiers …" Fragmar shook her head, totally confused by the need to weep and the sensation of laughter about to explode out of her. "I think our talk will be long enough, we should be comfortable." She raised her head and looked down the tunnel the way Ivy had come, then took a long, deep sniff. No sense of Elysto among all the dampness and stone and water creatures. "Is he with you? Waiting above ground?"

"He's run away to sulk. Just like he did when my parents married. I thought the whole rule about virgins and unicorns was some silly story or even a lie, to scare boys away."

"It was, at the beginning." She got up and gestured with a turn of her head for Ivy to follow. "Most unicorns are very warlike, and it was frustrating for them when they spent years turning a maiden into a weapon, and then have her go soft on them. And fat. Just because they fell in love and got themselves pregnant. A woman's fierceness turns in a completely different direction, once she's had a child. Well, one of the unicorn mages got fed up with what he considered wasted effort. So he created the spell to punish both sides, if a girl lost her focus and her discipline and her unicorn mentor allowed it. It's like an allergic reaction, multiplied in on itself, for the unicorn."

"Any loss of warrior skills and focus, for the girl?" Ivy asked.

"I'm not sure. It all happened so long ago, and the totally ironic part is that the allergic reaction in the unicorns took a great deal of the fighting spirit out of them. Too many of them became pretty boys and pursued poetry and posing for painters and dancing in the moonlight." She shuddered, which earned a sputter of laughter from the girl as she stepped up on the rock ledge on the other side of the little stream. "Please don't tell me Elysto --"

"Father said he was rather brutal and temperamental until I was born. Then he made himself my guardian." She rolled her eyes, eliciting a chuckle from Fragmar. "He and Mother were just starting to mend things between them when she made her attempt on the castle. Hafbaek seemed to have a spiritual awakening. He was filling the castle with prophets and teachers of the holy writ and seeking the Unseen. We all thought he was scared and trying to break from Fidus." She sighed. "Mother thought the spell enclosing the wood was weakening, but it must have been an illusion or trick of Fidus. She went in and … never came out. But she must have done something, because I got this."

She paused and started to untie the lacing down the front of her shirt, then looked around the shadowy tunnel. "I'll have to show you in the daylight. It's a scar. Like a great, sick, nearly naked tree. Its roots are over my heart and the branches go up to my collar bone. Father thinks she did something to the tree. Then Fidus and Hafbaek tightened their hold on things, and added more poison to what they've been throwing at the tree all these years." Her voice caught and broke and her shoulders slumped, visible despite the shadows of the tunnel.

<div align="center">~~~~~</div>

Fragmar had precious little to offer Ivy to eat. She did have some Human food, just not much variety. Much of it was liquid. Those who brought tribute in thanks for advice in the past had often left casks of wine. She used to trade it for more useful things, like parchment and ink and glue to repair books. Alcohol did not react kindly with her inner fires, though she knew plenty of dragons who loved the inner explosions. The far northern dragons had regular belching competitions and championships. She had meat to offer Ivy, and little else. The merchants she contacted provided live food beasts in exchange for her gold. Fragmar let them run wild, because she just could not bring herself to share living quarters with something she intended to eventually eat. She and Ivy both laughed when the girl broached one of the casks of wine and found it so old it didn't even qualify as vinegar. It served very nicely to help clean the tarnish from old metal cups and plates and jewelry.

As Ivy prepared her dinner, Fragmar told her what she knew about the fall of the Green Lady and the Horned King, and what she guessed from Fidus' reputation and history. She even related the ill-fated attempt to drop Elysto on the tree throne.

After dark, Fragmar and Ivy went out into the desert and sat on the sands, still hot from the day's baking. They talked as the winds turned cool and then chill as the night deepened.

"The most important part of Mother's quest into the castle was to determine if the tree was still alive. Then, once she determined its condition, she would try to break the spell of the poison. She determined over years of feints and questioning Hafbaek's soldiers and advisors that the spell was part of the castle walls, to keep pulling up poison from the surrounding, dying countryside, and send it seeping toward the tree."

Ivy wrapped her arms around her legs, clutching them to her chest, and her gaze turned dark and distant.

"She always insisted that the magic we could both feel in the castle meant the tree was still alive, and fighting. The spell would go to sleep once it had accomplished its purpose and killed the tree, and finally put the land into Fidus' thrall." She turned her head to Fragmar. "Or was she wrong?"

"It makes quite a bit of sense," the dragon said. She refrained from asking why Vivian had done it alone. Yes, she understood that it was much easier sneaking one person into an enemy castle than a band of fighters, but how could Vivian have thought that she could break through all in her own power?

Perhaps that was a remnant of the heart sickness Fidus had inflicted on Vivian and Cornagar. She still believed she was right, and able to do things that no one else could, and she didn't need help from anyone.

"I felt it when she died," Ivy whispered. "I was sick, and spent days half-asleep, caught in nightmares. Elysto took what I said in my delirium and what he felt vibrating through the land, and decided she sacrificed herself, deliberately. She was caught, or she realized she wouldn't be able to get away, and she ... my mother buffered the tree with her own blood. Diluting the poison, if she couldn't cure it completely. At least I know the tree is still alive."

"Oh, believe me, no matter how long it lingers and suffers and weakens, we will all feel the shattering of the roots of the world when the tree throne dies," Fragmar said.

Ivy met her gaze and understanding passed silently between them.

She sighed and pursed her lips in thought for a few seconds, then took a deep breath and seemed to brace herself to go on. "A year or two after ... some of our men managed to get into the castle far enough to look around, try to find a door to the other side. All the windows that look inward are high in the walls, so no one can ever see what is held prisoner there. And second," her voice dropped to a whisper, "the glass in those windows is stained red, as if painted with blood."

"What brings you here, beside seeking the true story?" Fragmar asked after the silence flowed between them, washing away the hints of fear and sorrow in the air.

"The poison is winning. The few trees I have contact with inside the castle are dying. I have to try to get into the castle and reach the tree." Ivy rubbed the spot on her breastbone. "My hope is that the scar Mother sent me is a connection, a way for me to get past the poison. If I can't heal the tree altogether, I can at least buy it time until we're strong enough to drive Hafbaek out of the castle and tear the walls down." She took a deep breath and sat up, releasing the legs she clasped tight to her chest. "I need your help, to learn everything ever written about Heartwood and my mother, her power, her gifts, the deeds she performed to defend the forest. Elysto said she forgot much, or lost much of herself, and that was why she failed. I need to regain that knowledge if I'm going to break through."

"That ... sounds like a good plan." Fragmar later laughed at herself, for flinching away from the spark of angry, determined light in Ivy's eyes. When could she make the girl understand that Heartwood required two guardians? Until the partnership between the Horned King and the Green Lady could be mended, the healing and release of the tree throne would only be part of the solution.

But that had to be a good place to start.

One step at a time. Maybe when the tree throne is freed, Cornagar's temperament will sweeten. He always was an arrogant little boy at heart.

~~~~~

Ivy stayed with Fragmar for a moon, researching everything recorded about the Heartwood, the tree throne, the Green Lady, and Fidus. She didn't want to know anything about the Horned King, except the signs of his approach. Her mother didn't trust Cornagar. Several times, she had thrashed his rude emissaries with her hair. When they persisted in their demands and condemnation, roots had sprung up from the ground and pulled them down, burying them alive. Ivy had found some of the letters brought by the emissaries, and they were full of anger, placing all the blame for the fall of the Heartwood on Vivian. She fully believed Cornagar would block her and do all he could to make her mission fail. If anyone was going to restore the Heartwood to its former glory, he had written in one
~~~~~

letter, it was going to be him. The Green Lady would have no part of it, no praise, and no power.

Fragmar tried only once to suggest that Ivy try to contact Cornagar, to make peace. It took two to rule the Heartwood, so common sense said it would take two to heal it.

"He wouldn't listen even if I did try to make peace," the girl had said. She glanced up from the long, dusty scroll she had been struggling to translate. "His men are all bandits and murderers. His son is even worse, from all the tales." She shuddered and wrapped her arms around herself, which let the scroll start to roll up. "Thank you, Unseen, I escaped that trap."

"What trap?" Fragmar fought down a surge of fire inside. Elysto should have kept her informed of all the bickering between Vivian and Cornagar's followers all these years.

"They kidnapped me when I was maybe five years old. Right after Mother died. The old bear claimed he was going to raise me properly, so I'd be a decent partner for his son when we were grown, and take back the tree throne. He said if Mother hadn't been a squirmy, picky, flighty idiot who thought there was magic in being a virgin, maybe they would have held onto the tree throne." She slapped her hands flat on the scroll, holding it down again, and turned to Fragmar, eyes wide. "How could they rule together for centuries and not ... not be ... I have to agree with the old bear in that regard, at least. They were partners, but they weren't ... *partners*. Completely united." She sighed. "Not like me and Bowen." A softening of her mouth, a warming in her eyes, told Fragmar all she needed to know about Ivy and the man in her life. "Not like Mother and my father. It nearly killed him when she died. That's the way marriage should be, don't you think? United in everything, body and soul and mind and ... everything."

"I agree totally."

"But that's not how Cornagar wanted it, or how it would have been if he had forced me to mate his son. That's not partnership. That's not how the Unseen wanted things for them, or for anyone."

Fragmar wished she were smaller, gentler, so she could have held Ivy and comforted the girl, while she still had that aching, lonely look in her eyes. Before she could think of a spell that might help her become briefly human, the moment passed. Ivy's jaw stiffened and new determination wiped away all signs of a little girl who had wept into her blankets, begging the Unseen to return her mother.

Neither said anything more on that regard, and Fragmar didn't bring up the subject of Cornagar again. In fact, she was rather disgusted with him. If he blamed Vivian for the fall of the Heartwood, then she could very easily imagine his idea of a "proper" partner for his son. Ivy would have been trained to let the men do the thinking and abdicate all responsibility for her soul and body. That was not how the Unseen had meant people to be, how they were designed to interact and work together. Even a dragon who had yet to find her soulmate could understand that.

Ivy left with a thick sheaf of papers full of bits of prophecies and helpful information. Fidus' past conquests. The few times he had been either driven away or his poisonous influence had been diluted. She regularly sent messages asking for more information, or gifts of books that hadn't helped her, but she thought Fragmar might be able to use to help others. Ivy had to delay her plan to infiltrate Hafbaek's castle when she discovered she was with child.

She named her daughter Aella. Fragmar laughed and wept just three tears, when Ivy admitted in a letter that she had let Elysto make himself the baby's guardian. The implication that he would ensure she avoided her mother's mistakes, starting with falling in love, was unmistakable. It would have been less obvious if he had written his intentions in stone with the tip of his horn.

~~~~~

At the end of three years, news came that Fidus was returning to reinforce the poison leaching into the Heartwood. If he needed to reinforce the castle walls, then perhaps the Heartwood was recovering and fighting back? Perhaps it could break free of its imprisonment?

Much as she loathed doing it, over the years Fragmar had paid attention to the rumors of the men who followed Cornagar and his son. She needed to be ready if they decided to act against Ivy and her followers. What she would do to persuade Cornagar to change his mind and tactics, she wasn't sure. She would follow her heart when the time came. And Cornagar wouldn't like it, whatever she did.

The rumors and reports gave no indication he had ever made any effort to free the Heartwood. Ivy, her father and husband and their followers had done little, besides a few self-destructive attempts to break through the poisoned wall to the tree throne. No one had made any efforts to bring healing to the torn partnership, to start the healing in the land.
~~~~~

Fidus had done his job well, dividing the Green Lady and the Horned King from each other, so Heartwood fell. Common sense said Cornagar's heir and Vivian's heir needed to unite to bring healing. The Unseen had made them to rule together, so neither one could break down the walls and free the Heartwood by themselves.

Then, seemingly in reaction to the impending return of Fidus, Agar, Cornagar's son led a gang of men to try to kidnap Ivy's daughter, Aella. He had an infant son now, and clearly, he hadn't learned from his father's mistakes, except to believe he could succeed where Cornagar had failed. The raid failed. Agar and most of his men died, leaving that innocent child to be raised by his resentful, angry grandfather. Where the mother was, no one knew. Just like no one knew what happened to the woman who gave Cornagar his son.

Fragmar briefly toyed with the idea of stealing the baby, to raise herself. The chances of surviving the attempt were small. Plus, the thought of raising an infant of any species terrified her.

Years went by. Hafbaek's grandson now sat on the throne, more madman than tyrant. People fled the kingdom in droves. Rumors said strange, warped beasts roamed the forests and ravaged the abandoned farmsteads and villages.

Then Elysto came stomping down the water tunnel to her fortress, snorting and shooting sparks and gusting flames. He burst out into the courtyard and stomped and reared, huffing in fury and drowning out Fragmar's polite greeting.

"It's all your fault. I can't stop her. She's been an idiot since the day that hulking nitwit smiled at her. What is it about giving birth that steals all the brains from a girl?"

He went on in that vein for nearly an hour. Fragmar surreptitiously plugged her ears with several large candles she had on hand, for when she was feeling poorly and couldn't generate enough magic light to read by. She closed two of her inner eyelids so she didn't have to see him clearly, and fell into a half-doze until he stopped pacing and shooting flames from nostrils and his horn. Then she dug her ears clear and waited until he quieted some more.

"You've said so much, so many ways, I'm not sure what you said," she said at last, when Elysto's glare, which had terrified Gorgons in the past, softened to the point of angry pleading.

For a few seconds, flames returned to his eyes, then he slumped and lowered his head and exhaled loudly, so nothing was left but steam.

"The idiot girl has taken everything the two of you have been researching all these years, and she is going to try to puncture the castle wall. If she can disrupt the flow of the poison, then she can weaken Hafbaek. Maybe by the time Aella is grown, the castle can be overthrown."

"Isn't Hafbaek dead?"

"They name their sons after themselves." Elysto shrugged. "Humans. They seem to think they're immortal if they pass on the name."

"Well, they certainly pass on their madness."

"Truth." He snorted and looked up at her. "I've missed you, as insane as that seems."

"You know where I am."

"Yes, but that wall of silence you hold around yourself just gets thicker, stronger with the years."

"And you're too busy protecting your precious virgin to look beyond your own walls."

"Hmm, truth as well." Another sigh. "Fragmar, what are we going to do? She's going to kill herself just like Vivian did. And that idiot Cornagar just makes things worse."

"We need to bash their heads together until they apologize." Fragmar sighed. "Vivian and Cornagar could have fixed things years ago, if they had just apologized, instead of blaming each other."

"Truth."

The night let out a silent shriek of a kind Fragmar hoped never to endure again. Land and sky separated. The moons dimmed and a foul, hot stink blew across them. Fragmar dug her talons into the sand, into the bedrock beneath her fortress, and felt the trembling in the land. It came from leagues away.

It came from the Heartwood.

The silence was death.

The land mourned, and for a brief, aching moment, it tried to die as well.

The silence throbbed and deafened in that heartbreaking pause just after a lush forest bursts into flame, or the moment after a dying elk lets out his last furious roar of defiance and submits to defeat, releasing his last breath, knowing there will be no more.

"No, no, no, no!" Elysto roared. He reared back and fire erupted from his horn and nostrils. He spun three times on his rear legs, then he leaped into the cave mouth, and the echoes of his racing hooves came back down the water tunnel.

Fragmar hunkered down, pressing herself into the sand, feeling the devastation in the land through the bedrock. She held her breath as the awful, shredded, shattered silence faded back into the normal silence that felt like a balm and shield. She listened to the throbbing of pain in the land, and she felt the slow sting as poison slid outward across the stolen kingdom.

Ivy had succeeded in breaking the wall of Hafbaek's castle, but she hadn't prevented the poison from drowning the Heartwood. She had merely released poison to flow outward as well as inward to the tree throne. It seeped across the landscape, the devastated meadows and the open ground where primeval forests had once ruled. The castle hadn't fallen when she breached the wall. Hafbaek's heirs still held the land. Still the dupes of Fidus.

And Vivian's heir was dead, killed in the attempt to undo her mother's foolishness and mend the betrayal.

The reaction of the land showed how close Ivy had come to healing it, and that was the bitterest blow of all. There had been no reaction when Vivian died in her attempt to reach the tree throne, showing just how much she had become separated from the remains of Heartwood.

Fragmar mourned until she thought her tears would quench her inner fires for all time.

Eight years later, Kosta, Ivy's father, came to Fragmar. Not to blame her for the research that led to Ivy's attempt, but because he had found the letters Fragmar had sent and realized she was his daughter's friend and had tried to warn her what would and wouldn't work.

"And yes," he admitted, with a tired, dry chuckle, "it took me this long to accept that there are friendly dragons. And scholarly dragons. Thanks to the damage Fidus has done, most magical creatures only have two choices. Flee to the wastelands Humans don't want, or ally with the despots, trading freedom for some security."

Fragmar nodded and waited in silence for him to emerge from the thoughtful, introspective light in his eyes. She had tried to keep track of the fates of magical creatures throughout the world, after this latest devastation. The slow death of Heartwood affected all magical creatures, no matter how far away. Many wise beasts chose to retreat within themselves, either in fear or sorrow, and became little more than dumb creatures. Nowadays, the only visible magical creatures were the monsters. Fragmar supposed she had survived because she was so quiet she was nearly invisible, and no threat. After all, how could someone whose advice was constantly ignored be considered a threat?

"I have heard so many stories," she said, when he finally stirred again and reached for the cup of ale she had been pleased to offer him in hospitality. It amused her a little that Kosta didn't seem to notice the cup was made of gold and crusted with emeralds. "Can you tell me what happened?"

"She was betrayed, and we were fools. We took in some men who claimed they had fled Hafbaek's growing madness. They waited more than a year, proving themselves loyal. And all that time, they reported to Hafbaek and prepared a trap." He choked and took a long draft from the cup. "Ivy, Bowen, nearly all their men … slaughtered. That lunatic unicorn …" Kosta snorted and managed a crooked, brief grin. "Skewered most of the traitors, skewered a good dozen of Hafbaek's men. Didn't do any good. They were outnumbered. Cornagar and his men were waiting and attacked the few who escaped. They only fought Hafbaek's men to protect their own filthy necks." He took another gulp and slapped the cup down on the stone step next to him. The gold rang and crumpled from the impact. "But Elysto skewered Hafbaek and his brute son, and for that I can nearly forgive him for what he's done since!"

"Oh, no," she whispered. "What did he do?"

"He has Aella."

"What do you mean, he has her?"

Elysto took charge of Ivy's daughter. Kosta remarked that he wished the unicorn had stormed Hafbaek's castle while it was in chaos and stole the madman's toddler grandson, now the nominal ruler. Elysto wouldn't let anyone near the girl when she wasn't sitting on his back. While a maiden riding a unicorn was a powerful rallying point for the people now suffering as their land continued to slowly die, Kosta feared for his granddaughter. The weight of her heritage had crushed Ivy and driven her to trusting men she barely knew. How would being raised by a unicorn make things even harder for Aella? What could Elysto be teaching her?

Fragmar tried to find out. In a dozen attempts, she only spotted him twice. Both times he gave her looks of killing fury, reared back and fled into the darkness of the trees. Clearly, Elysto blamed

Fragmar for Ivy's tragic defeat and death.

She blamed herself. What could she have told Ivy differently? Why didn't she lecture until the silly girl understood that she wasn't going to oust Hafbaek and defeat Fidus until she remedied Vivian's error and made peace with Cornagar?

Maybe she should find Cornagar and his grandson, and pound some sense and humility into their stubborn heads? Yet, she knew too well, and with some bitterness: peace didn't come from one side imposing their beliefs on another. There was no peace when coercion reigned. There would never be peace until the Unseen took the higher seat at the conference table, and all others willingly gave up their goals and desires in submission. Willingly, not forced.

Recalling how Cornagar had been when he was still the Horned King, Fragmar wondered why he hadn't lashed out at Vivian centuries earlier, insisting on everything being done his way. Perhaps Fidus had been so successful because he had found deep, fertile ground for his seeds of discontent and resentment in both former rulers of the Heartwood.

Perhaps Elysto had the right of it. Separating Aella from those who supported Vivian and Ivy's beliefs and goals was the first step in planting the seeds of necessary change.

Perhaps separating that little boy from his grandfather's influence was the first step in creating a Horned King who would do whatever was necessary to heal the land.

Fragmar had a long talk with the Unseen about it. Of course, she had to trust that the Unseen was listening. The hard part was waiting for an answer. Perhaps the hardest part was preparing herself for an answer she might not entirely like.

So she almost laughed when, five years later, she heard that conflict and rebellion had torn apart Cornagar's bandit tribe. His sub-chiefs had taken their loyal followers and each went their own way. Cornagar had raged until he collapsed and died. His grandson had vanished. No one knew if he was dead or alive, if he had been rescued by a loyal follower or turned over to Hafbaek for a reward.

Fragmar shuddered at the revelation that requests made to the Unseen were indeed heard and answered. She needed to be more careful of what exactly she asked for.

The years passed, and the watered lands encroached further on her desert. Caravans passed within earshot of her fortress often enough to become a nuisance. The thudding of horses' and donkey's hooves, or the braying of camels, the shouts of men and the creaking of wagons grew too loud and lasted too long while they trudged past. Fragmar ached for the moons of quiet, broken only by the wind hissing across the sand. She had to face an unpleasant truth: sooner or later, someone would believe the tales of the dragon in the fortress, and then invade her sanctuary, looking for treasure. She had plenty of treasure, but not the kind those invaders would want. Disappointing the selfish and greedy always led to trouble. She was just too tired and too busy studying to fight them off. If she wanted to preserve her peace and quiet, the time had come to abandon her cozy, dry fortress.

There were no people within one hundred leagues of Spearpoint Summit. For the sake of solitude, she could spare enough magic to drive away the damp. She wore herself out, taking nearly a moon of nights to fly cartloads of her books and scrolls and tablets to her cave.

She devoted herself to digging through the heart of the mountain to create ventilation that pulled away the damp air and brought in dry air, to preserve her books and scrolls. The project took years, interspersed with reorganizing her library, and occasional trips to the outside world to rebuild her food herds left behind in the desert, and to try to gather news. Fortunately, the new generation of would-be heroes were more interested in knowledge and plumbing the secrets of the universe. For power, naturally, but they were willing to sit down and talk rather than fight, when a dragon flew down to their encampment or the courtyard of a castle containing a wise man, in search of information. Fragmar was more than willing to trade what she considered useless information about hidden treasure hoards for news of the world.

Despite her caution in approaching Humans far from her lair, word spread: a dragon inhabited Spearpoint Summit. She adjusted her reconstruction of the heart of the mountain to make her labyrinth even more confusing and tumble unwanted visitors into noxious mud or pits filled with spiders or roaches.

Elysto arrived when she had barely begun the project, and terrified her with his furious snorts and stamps, the scraping squeal of his hooves and horn on the stone tunnel, and worst of all, his wails of agonized dismay.

"What am I doing wrong?" he roared, when he finally emerged into the cavern in the bowels of the mountain.

He stopped short, looking around with some wonder and a little admiration. The echoes from his hooves stomping down the curving tunnel finally died away. The multitude of crystalline stalactites reflected sound and light. Fragmar had some pride in how well the plan had unfolded, guiding the accelerated dripping of water, selecting which minerals would flow in that water, and adding some heat at the right moments to control the thousands of shiny, jewel-toned teeth coming from the ceiling. She only needed a dozen oil lamps, placed at strategic intervals around the perimeter of her massive cavern for optimum reflection. Everything was lit properly for reading, with a reduced risk of fires.

"Nice. If you like silence." He huffed. "Which I know you do. And you know I wouldn't interrupt your precious silence if it wasn't important."

"What is Aella doing now?"

"It's not her, it's her fool daughter. What is wrong with me that I can't raise these girls to keep their eyes on the goal and stop falling in love?" he roared.

Fragmar choked, trying not to laugh.

"You have to help me stop her eloping. This one is the worst of all. He's so … so poetic. How can a man be a skilled warrior if he's crammed so many poems into his head? He's disgusting!"

"Would he be so disgusting if she wasn't the Green Lady's heir?"

That stopped him in his furious pacing across the width of the cavern. He skidded, so his hooves squeaked on the smoothed stone floor. She waited as he turned around and came back to her, his steps slower than heartbeats, soft, as if each raised and lowered footstep was an effort of will.

"You have to help me. She used to listen to me, but then she just stopped, and she lets him pour his sticky, silly verses and pretty words into her ears and … I should have listened to my gut years ago and brought her to you," he said, when she could see his dark, wide, sorrowful eyes.

"Why me?"

He snorted, shook his head so his ebony mane fell into his eyes and then swept it aside again. "Girl buries herself in books. You'd swear she was your daughter, not Aella's." His voice cracked a little, and Fragmar heard the pain still associated with her name.

"What happened to Aella?"

"That boy didn't die when Cornagar's band of idiot brutes split apart. The ones who raised him taught him that rulers stand alone, they don't share, and that was his grandfather's downfall. Sharing the tree throne. Only one can sit in the tree throne, not two."

"True, but the tree throne was never for the Green Lady and the Horned King."

"They've forgotten that part. Or maybe they've convinced themselves that was the reason they fell."

"Wanting to sit on the throne, letting Fidus convince them they wouldn't be happy until they took the tree throne for themselves, not sharing it, and certainly not kneeling before it. That was how they fell." Fragmar shuddered, imagining the tree throne, like a massive hand, suddenly clenching and enclosing anyone who dared to claim the seat. Squeezed until their magic had been wrenched from them, and then throwing them away, out of the Heartwood.

"That doesn't really matter right now, does it?" A bit of his old temper returned, just for a few seconds, a few green and red sparks in his eyes and coming from his nose.

"It will matter someday."

"Hmph. True."

"So Cornagar's heir attacked, intent on killing Aella instead of enslaving her?"

"That's the short end of the tale." He nodded. "Fragmar, you have to help me."

"How? Swoop down on them, carry her away, terrify her to stop her eloping?"

He stopped short, his mouth open for a few seconds. His beard was lopsided, and she had the sudden, awful suspicion he had been chewing on it. That was a very bad sign.

Elysto's eyes lit up. He grinned, baring his fangs.

"Would you?"

So that was what they did.

And just in time, too.

Aella's daughter, River, had sneaked away from her guards and walked for nearly half an hour to a meadow filled with moonlight. It was a very bad place for a tryst, from Fragmar's point of view. The shadows of the trees surrounding the meadow were black, thick like old honey, and could easily hide movement. Such as archers shooting from hiding. What was the fool girl doing, making a target of herself, coming out into the open a good dozen paces?

Fragmar set Elysto down when they reached the forest camp of River and her followers, then landed on a cliff that formed a wall on the long side of the meadow. Opposite the cliff face was a river. That left only two directions to run in an ambush. Fragmar crouched down on the cliff face, to present as low a profile as possible, and watched River pace back and forth. At least she had the sense not to stand still and make an easy target of herself. Elysto was right, the girl had lost half her common sense and all the training he had given her, when she fell in love.

Not that Fragmar would ever admit it, but Elysto might have something there, insisting that maiden warriors stay virgins. Or at least stay far away from smooth-talking, handsome poets.

Now the unicorn came puffing up the steep slope from behind her, and settled down on the flat surface next to her.

"There he is," he whispered. "You can smell him coming. Disgusting."

Fragmar took a deep breath, and caught the aroma of spicy, musky oils. He was right. The scent was so thick it was nearly overpowering. Why would a man wear such a strong scent … unless he was trying to cover up something? Bad washing habits? Sickness?

Or maybe drugs, intended to fuddle the mind of the girl who inhaled them? It made sense. She had read of many love potions that weren't swallowed by the target but worn by the hunter. They were usually applied with incantations to allow the wearer to take over the mind of the one who inhaled the scents.

She told Elysto her theory. He growled and a deep, dark red glow grew at the base of his horn and far inside his nostrils.

"Don't set the woods on fire just yet," she whispered. "The scent could be covering something else."

"Can't smell anything but that stink. It's been infiltrating the entire camp since the day he arrived. You need to smell for me."

"I'm trying, believe me. Now hush so we can hear what they're saying."

The two trysting sweethearts were whispering, their heads close together. Fragmar couldn't hear anything but hisses and murmurs. No clear words. At least they weren't kissing, and River didn't put her arms around the man. Odd. It looked more like she was leading him on a little chase, twisting aside or stepping back every time he tried to put his arms around her. Was the girl a tease? Or … could it be she didn't trust him? But if she didn't, then why was she meeting him here?

Then Fragmar recognized an odor rising up through the man's

overpowering perfume. She trembled, knowing that salty tang like the sea was dangerous, but she couldn't quite put her talon on --

"They're surrounded," she whispered.

The sea tang came from men who had been creeping up through the forest to blockade the meadow. It was a trap.

"Meet me at my cave," she told Elysto, and leaped before he could respond.

She dove, silent, talons extended. Her hind feet hit the ground and she snatched up River with her forepaws. Pivoting, she swept her tail across the nearby trees, snapping them off near the ground and sending a dozen bowmen flying, shrieking in mortal terror. A heartbeat later she leaped skyward again. She kicked off crooked and sent the treacherous sweetheart flying, to smash into a tree. As she gained altitude, up above the cliff top with just a few beats of her wings, the man shrieked. She looked down in time to see flames erupt from Elysto's nose as he skewered the man a second time.

River didn't struggle. She lay quiet, but stiff in Fragmar's paws, neatly caged from head to foot. Considering that the girl had been at least partially raised by Elysto, Fragmar was surprised she didn't struggle or curse or display some fit of temper. She knew better than to expect River to be in a good mood when she released her, more than an hour later, deep inside the safety of her cavern.

"You ruined a perfectly good trap," River spat, as she stomped away from Fragmar. She stopped after a dozen steps, turned to face her, and the two glared into each other's eyes for a few heartbeats. Then a vicious grin cracked the girl's long, sharp-boned face. "If I knew where to find you, I would have asked you to do just what you did."

"They were surrounding you on both sides," Fragmar said. "Bydensi mercenaries. The smell of the sea is very distinctive, part of their strength rituals."

"Oh, so that's who they were ..." She nodded. "What are the chances they're in Hafbaek's service and not the little Thorn's?"

"Who is the little Thorn?"

"Gracious, the Horned King's heir. I call him the little Thorn because that's all he can do. Poke little holes, cause some irritation." She turned around, her smile softening as she studied the massive cavern with its crystals and stalactites and lanterns and tall shelves and tables filled with books. "I lost hope when I heard you had abandoned your desert fortress. Hugh has been trying to find you, but … This is amazing."

"River, don't you realize that you probably would have died tonight, or at least become a prisoner?"

"My men were close enough to --"

"No, they weren't, you ninny," Elysto shouted, his voice coming down a tunnel. "Most of your men were ambushed before they got within a hundred paces of the meadow." The clatter of his hooves echoed to them. He had chosen the spiral tunnel to enter. Fragmar wasn't about to tell him about the shorter, more direct tunnel. Let the old grump stew a little. She decided she liked this girl and wanted some time with her without his interference.

"Oh." River went a little pale. She crossed her arms over her chest and nodded slowly. "Then I should thank you."

Fragmar snorted, amused at the "should" inserted in there. Meaning the girl was much like Ivy, unwilling to admit when she was wrong, yet wise enough to recognize when she had made a mistake.

"Suppose you tell us when you discovered your sweetheart was bait, and how long you had this plan in motion to stop him. I assume you wanted to find out who hired him?" Fragmar looked around for a chair to offer the girl. She had prepared for Human visitors, on the off chance that one would arrive who she would invite into her lair, but she couldn't remember where she had put the furniture.

River found a bench by the time Elysto joined them. The story was easy enough to guess. It was almost a waste of time for her to tell it, but Fragmar calculated that Elysto needed to hear it, to prove River hadn't betrayed all her training, hadn't been so blinded by romance and poetry she had betrayed *him*. It was the poetry, the fancy words, and the overpowering scent that made River doubt the man. She had her doubts about his reputation as a soldier, his skill and bloodthirstiness. So she had sent couriers and her most trusted advisor, a scholarly man named Hugh, to investigate. They found that the man who went with the name was real. His reputation was real. But the man who had come to her wearing the name was not the man. The hero had been ambushed and taken prisoner more than seven moons ago.

River got as far as saying that Hugh had found the real hero, and sent her word about his rescue, when several alarm spells went off at once. They were set at the mouths of all the tunnels leading down into the heart of the mountain. Fragmar had illusions set all around the mountain, so it should have been impossible for more than one warning spell to be set off, or one doorway to a tunnel to be breached. For all the alarm spells to go off at once meant --

"Treachery," she snapped. "Someone is using magic to track you, River."

The young woman stood and held out a hand to Elysto. "Is there a spell on me? How can there be? You warded me."

"Probably that stink he slathered himself with is a spell that needs time to settle in," the unicorn snarled. He stomped over to River and raised his head. "Hold on tight. Might get hot."

"You killed him too quickly," she snapped, and grabbed hold of his spiraling horn with both hands. She didn't wince as the sharp edges cut her palms.

Fragmar sighed. Definitely, Elysto had had too much influence over this girl.

A sickly yellow glow melted through her sleeve. River cursed and let go of Elysto's horn, tugged up her sleeve, and pulled an ornate gold band off her arm. It glowed brighter.

"Drop it," Elysto barked.

River obeyed, and he stomped on it, sending a sharp ringing echo through the cavern. The metal didn't bend, despite the multiple blows of his hoof. Elysto cursed as the ringing grew louder, sharper, clashing more as it echoed multiple times. He cursed again and thrust down with his horn. The sharp tip pierced the armband and it shattered with a scream like a flock of harpies. Poison yellow light burst out through the cavern.

A second round of alarm spells went off, as invaders penetrated farther down the tunnels.

Flames spun out from the light and settled on the shelves and the tables piled high with books and scrolls. The echoes continued, and stalactites broke off, plummeting down. Fragmar spread her wings to shield River and Elysto, and grunted as spikes of rock slammed into her back and head.

"This way!" She pointed to a side tunnel that she intended to use to funnel snowmelt down to a cistern she hadn't started to dig yet. It was nearly straight, and emerged higher than any other tunnel on the mountain.

Elysto surged ahead of her and raced up the incline. She caught up River and put her on her back, in between several spine ridges. River had the sense to lie down, wedge herself in tightly, and hold on as Fragmar raced up the incline on all fours.

The invaders coming down that tunnel had the longest way to go, and were few in number. Elysto shot flames at them and roared fury from mouth and horn as he raced at them. The idiots didn't have the sense to flee. He skewered one, burned another, and knocked two aside with wide sweeps of his head as he knocked the skewered man off his horn. Then he was through, and Fragmar stomped on the ones who were moving.

~~~~~

Fragmar didn't have time to sit and mourn her library, her centuries of scholarship and collecting and arranging, and especially her lovely silence and solitude. Once they emerged from the mountain, she triggered all her avalanche spells, turning her mountain into a tomb. Then she caught up Elysto and flew back to River's camp. The mercenaries hadn't attacked the camp, focusing all their attention on the tracking spell in the armband. They were all dead, trapped inside the burning mountain. There was no guarantee that more Bydensi mercenaries didn't remain free and above ground, preparing to attack. Fragmar landed and had to fend off a hailstorm of arrows and crossbow bolts. Then she had to knock aside, as gently as possible, a dozen men who were so intent on rescuing River, they didn't hear her shouting that Fragmar was an ally. Once River got them to listen, the men showed their good sense and they began the task of packing up the camp and moving far away.

River's parents and grandparents had prepared half a dozen strongholds to retreat to, if their enemies ever located them. Fragmar provided transportation for the wounded and ill and took them immediately to the one River chose for their new home. She went back to her mountain to free her herds to whatever fate awaited them, and checked that all the avalanches were effectively blocking all the tunnels out of the mountain. From the lack of sound and sense of movement, and lack of smoke, she suspected the men had either been crushed in the avalanches that effectively sealed her cavern, or they had smothered in the smoke of the fires. She tried to find some solace in her library dying such a worthy death, but she couldn't.

When she returned to River's new stronghold, she found a quiet spot on a high plateau overlooking the warren of small canyons and caves. There she mourned in silence, with tears that raised a cloud of steam. That steam brought Hugh to her, the one-legged, one-eyed man who had turned to scholarship when he was injured in
~~~~~

childhood. He had been River's closest friend and had sacrificed himself to protect her in a kidnapping attempt. Elysto was fond of him, but Fragmar found it amusing that he referred to Hugh as "the boy," when the man was a full head taller than River, with wide shoulders and a steady stride despite his crutch and peg leg.

She found it especially amusing when she caught the sweet glances of silent communication River and Hugh exchanged, and Elysto never reacted. Either he didn't see, or he didn't want to see, because then he would have to drive Hugh away.

But that was later.

Hugh came to Fragmar that day, after letting her grieve in steamy silence for several hours. He carried a huge sack of books on his back. Fragmar calculated how much they had to weigh, and how hard a climb he had made with one leg, to reach her lookout point. He was quite admirable, this scholar who had pulled away the false identity and name of the Bydensi mercenary attempting to romance and kidnap or kill River.

"I know of a good dozen castles that have been abandoned, thanks to plagues and wars and the uprising of magical beasts with extremely bad tempers," he said, after unloading the pack of books. "All with intact libraries."

"Do you?" Her heart picked up its slogging, aching pace. She blinked away the last few steaming tears. "What condition are the books in?"

"As good as they can be, when there's only me and two others who know the spells to ward away damp and insects and fire. It takes a lot out of us to travel the circuit and refresh them, but we manage to visit each one at least once a year. I thought maybe … maybe it was time to collect them all in one place?" He offered her a smile that gave a hint of the mischievous, valiant boy he had been. If not for the scars raking the left side of his face, and that unbecoming eye patch, he would be quite handsome.

Her high opinion of River rose a few notches more. The girl was wise enough to see beyond the scars and the missing leg.

"Where should we put them?" she said, after thinking for several moments, and testing Hugh by making him wait.

He grinned.

Eventually, Elysto would catch on about what was already established between Hugh and River. He would fume. He would rail against Fragmar for encouraging the pairing. She imagined the cranky old unicorn scolding them all, and warning them that this time, he was washing his hooves of them all, and he wouldn't break his heart yet again by helping to raise River's daughter.

That suited Fragmar just fine. Perhaps Vivian and her descendants had been going about this all wrong. They didn't need a warrior to return the Green Lady to the tree throne. Perhaps what they needed was a bookish, scholarly girl. One who could talk sense into the Horned King's heir, wherever he might be. A girl who wouldn't strike him as a rival, who could charm him and show him the benefits of peaceful intentions, scholarship, and if necessary, guile and stealth.

Blessed Unseen, help me. I am mad enough to willingly sacrifice my solitude for the sake of the children who will restore the tree throne. There are some things more important than silence, I suppose.

End

THE HIDEAWAY
By Deborah Cullins Smith

1986

Alvin shifted into third gear as the road morphed from asphalt to a dirt road with more ruts than he'd remembered from his last trip. His handsome profile bordered on arrogant, and his sandy hair was sculpted into waves. The first thing one always noted when meeting him was the piercing blue eyes that mesmerized — unless one was foolish enough to cross him. At thirty-four years of age, Alvin was rising within his firm like a shooting star.

His companion, Sydney, was a voluptuous woman with raven hair, permed into loose curls that fell around her shoulders, and deep green eyes. Her green silk blouse billowed in the breeze from the open windows. Sunglasses hid most of her thin face, but Alvin knew she still suffered from the cocktails they had enjoyed at the hotel the night before. He had been fond of gin and tonic in his early days at the firm. Too fond. Then for a few years, he switched to straight tonic. One day he might allow himself to indulge again. His boss had liked whiskey neat. But too much drinking led to demotions and even terminations. Alvin's eyes narrowed. He was not going to fall by the wayside like so many others had done.

Sydney yelped as the car skidded into a deeper groove in the road, then leveled out again in Alvin's expert hands. The shiny red Camaro might bottom out here and there, but it had the muscle to take whatever this country road could dish out.

"How much more of this are we going to have to endure?" Sydney asked.

"Oh, it will be worth it, my dear," Alvin said with a short laugh. "You're going to love this little bed and breakfast. Very cozy, secluded."

"You've been here before?" she asked, suspicion in the green eyes that stared over the rim of her sunglasses.

"Heard about it from a friend at work," he said smoothly.

Her lips curved into a pouty smile, meant to beguile. "Didn't bring the little wife out here?"

Alvin sighed. "I've told you before, Sydney. My wife is a socialite with more money and standing than she knows what to do with. She wants a successful man to escort her to charity events, and I need her connections. Purely a business transaction."

He gritted his teeth and downshifted again. "Besides, what about your boyfriend? I heard he's been questioning your long work hours."

"*Ex*-boyfriend, love," Sydney simpered. "It's over between us. I've got all I need right here." She wove her left arm around Alvin's right bicep and shivered at the strength she felt beneath the linen dress shirt.

Alvin grinned at her and reached over to grip her knee possessively. She might not be the sharpest knife in the drawer, but she excelled in lovemaking. That was all that mattered this weekend.

The road leveled out, rounded a curve and Alvin hit third gear again. The faster they got to the inn, the better.

The road wove between tall oak trees so thick their branches met overhead. Sydney shivered as the sun disappeared behind the canopy of leaves. Then suddenly the rambling old house appeared on the left side of the road. Honeysuckle and tea roses sent green tendrils and tiny blooms lacing around the wide wraparound porch rails. Chairs and porch swings were scattered along the veranda, providing a welcome bit of respite.

"Oh, Alvin!" Sydney's mouth dropped open. "How lovely!"

"Oh, so you approve?" Alvin asked as he guided the car into the gravel parking lot beside the house.

"It's perfect," she whispered, following the words with a passionate kiss.

Stonework formed the base of the house, topped by ancient bricks and capped by a slate roof. The shutters were painted a light sky blue that exuded a welcome atmosphere.

Hollyhocks and large flagstones led from the parking area to the front of the building. Sydney stepped gingerly in her four-inch heels, squealing as her ankles wobbled on the uneven surfaces.

Alvin grabbed their bags from the trunk of the car, and Sydney grasped his arm as they approached the front door. An elderly man in an old-fashioned black suit greeted them at the entrance and motioned them inside with a graceful bow. Alvin gave his name and the gentleman proffered a large red registry and a quill pen. As the men completed the monetary formalities, Sydney glanced around the lobby, which contained some of the most beautiful antique furniture she'd ever seen. Colorful Persian rugs added a glow to the gleaming hardwood floors. Tiffany lamps graced mahogany end tables. A large grandfather clock reigned supreme over the entryway, and it gonged as the hour struck one o'clock in the afternoon. Newspapers were stacked neatly on coffee tables, and Victorian sofas and chairs clustered in small groupings through the first two rooms at the entry. An elegant dining room stretched off to the left with crystal chandeliers. It was filled with small tables, each seating only two.

"Not bad for a young executive, eh?" Alvin whispered in her ear, his arms snaking around her waist.

"M-m-m-m," she purred. "Not bad at all. But the real test is yet to come. Let's check out the bedroom."

A smile crinkled the corners of Alvin's eyes. "Whatever you say, love."

~~~~~

Almost midnight. The moon hung low in the sky.

No matter how many women Alvin had brought up here over the last few years, it never ceased to amaze him. Mesmerized by the quaint décor and homey touches, they never saw the end game until it was upon them. Alvin leaned against his car, raising a cigarette to his lips. He puffed out a long stream of smoke. Sydney still slept in the queen-sized bed. The room overlooked the back of the property, a densely wooded area with walking trails that led to a stable. They had never made it that far. Sydney's needy appetites kept them in the bedroom for most of the weekend. She had become far too possessive lately. That wouldn't do. She had overestimated her value to Alvin. In the beginning, he had enjoyed her vivacious company, but lately, it had become clear that she wanted more. When the word 'commitment' came up, Alvin knew it was time to end things. Gloria's purse strings were far too valuable to his goals. His wife tolerated his indiscretions, but only so far.

"I will not be made to look a fool, Alvin," she told him in the beginning. "You may keep your women if you want to, but I don't want to ever see it in the society column."

Alvin complied. He sighed. It was almost midnight.

~~~~~

In the darkness of the bedroom on the second floor, Sydney wakened with a jerk. She reached for Alvin's warm body, but he wasn't there. She sat up, her eyes searching the darkened room. Furniture loomed in the shadows like crouching monsters. Fear clutched at her, and small gasps left her lips as she sat up slowly. In the light of day, this room had been beautiful, but it had changed. As a grandfather clock in the lobby chimed out twelve, shadows lengthened. Wallpaper peeled from the walls and creatures scurried and scratched in the ceiling overhead.

Sydney felt like she'd been dropped into one of those haunted house horror movies. She clutched the clean bedsheets to her chest, only to realize she held a fistful of cobwebs. Shrieking, she wiped her hands on her short satin gown as she leapt from the bed.

"Alvin!" she screamed. She ran for the door, but the knob came off in her hand. She beat the wood panels with both hands until blood began to stream down her arms from the splinters piercing her like pins. "Alvin!"

She backed away from the door as horror mingled with disbelief. Large, lumbering footsteps echoed in the hallway. They stopped outside her door. Heavy breathing filled the room and choked the screams as Sydney began sobbing.

~~~~~

Alvin sighed and ground out the cigarette with the heel of his Italian loafer. He slid into the driver's seat and started the engine. He heard one last scream, "No-o-o-o-o-o! Al-l-l-l-vi-i-i-in!"

Shifting through the gears with lightning speed, Alvin headed back to New York City.

Alone.

Spring, 2020

> *Through a tunnel dark with trees,*
> *Lies a ramshackle house of sin*
> *Devours all who venture within...*

"I'm tellin' you, Mrs. Robbins, there ain't nothin' worth seein' down this road."

The squad car fishtailed on gravel. Alice gripped the door handle with one white-knuckled fist and braced herself from falling against the dashboard with the other arm extended and elbow
~~~~~

locked. She gritted her teeth in frustration and fought back burning tears. It had taken almost an hour to drive upstate from the city. The local sheriff had been adamant that this address was on private property. She was not to go poking around out there by herself. Then it had taken another hour to convince the grizzled Sheriff Hardwood to make the drive out to "The Hideaway." It was listed as a quaint bed and breakfast, far from the hustle and bustle of the city.

"My husband is missing, Sheriff." Alice's voice trembled. "This is the only lead I have as to where he might have gone."

A bone-jarring pothole sent Alice's head smashing against the roof of the car. She bit back a cry of pain.

"Sorry, ma'am," the sheriff said. "Just ain't no way to avoid these dad-gummed craters. Nobody's used this road for years. Not in this century anyway. Just no reason to spend money fixin' a road that nobody's gonna' use." He glanced at the attractive lady and wondered why a man would ever walk out on a good-looking woman like Alice Robbins.

Enormous oak trees clustered on both sides of the road, branches meeting overhead and blocking the darkening skies. If the ominous clouds had hidden the sun in town, out here beneath the ancient oaks, the skies disappeared entirely. Alice shivered despite the sticky August heat. The ad she'd found in her husband's jacket pocket had shown this tree-lined path leading to a charming Victorian structure, surrounded by gardens.

"A romantic getaway..." the ad had promised. But this road didn't feel romantic to Alice. Evil lived among these trees.

She drew in a sharp breath. The curved path straightened ahead of them, and the derelict remains of the B & B, which had obviously seen its heyday long before the Roosevelt years—Teddy Roosevelt, that is—loomed amid the trees. The path veered to a small driveway on the left side of the building. A wilted garden, overrun by weeds, wove around the house like a woman's necklace, almost hiding the sign with raised wooden letters bearing the name "The Hideaway."

"Just like I told you, ma'am," the sheriff said, pulling the car to a stop. "It's an old ruin. Nobody's lived here in almost a hundred years."

Alice frowned, squinting at the hint of dark grey metal hiding behind the tall red hollyhocks. Then she gasped and bolted from the squad car.

"Ma'am! Wait!" Hardwood threw open his own door and

lumbered after her. "This old place ain't safe, ma'am. You can't just poke around here. It'll fall down around your ears!"

Alice wasn't aiming for the heavy arched door. She stumbled toward the side of the building, tripping on the flagstones that wound through the flowerbeds. At one time, they must have been exquisite. Alice dodged bumblebees and thorny brambles, homing in on that glint of gunmetal grey.

"That's my husband's car!" she cried out as she ran.

Alice skidded to a halt; eyes widened. Her hand trembled as she reached out to touch the sleek Mercedes Benz C Class.

"It's Jackson's car," she stated, her voice unnaturally loud in the oppressive silence. "He was here, Sheriff. Maybe he's in the house." Her gaze rose from the car to the windows. Eyes of darkness—dread—pierced Alice's heart and she shivered. She peered through the tinted windows of the Mercedes and stifled a sharp cry.

Hardwood reached her side, his chest heaving as he sought to catch up to the distraught woman. He followed her line of sight and uttered a brief curse.

Alice's world spun, and blackness engulfed her.

Two Days Ago...

Leather-bound notepads and gold-plated ballpoint pens lined the mahogany table. Silk ties and tailor-made suits added elegance and style. These were the elite of New York's best and brightest financial stars. The stock market, real estate, investments, this was the top of the food chain, and these men and women had risen to the very pinnacle of success.

Alexander Pierce leaned to his left, catching a whiff of Chanel No. 5, and whispered to the impeccably groomed woman in designer silk.

"Plans for the weekend, Georgi?"

Georgeanna Helena Weston shifted to the right, burgundy painted lips twitching slightly behind the matching manicured nails. "Never mind, Alex. You're not invited."

Alex's gaze drifted to the hint of black lace between the lapels of Georgeanna's wine-colored suit, which hugged her curves like a second skin.

"Who is it this time, darling? The new office boy toy?" he whispered with a sly smile.

The ice in Georgeanna's stare should have frozen the fire in his veins, but his own extracurricular activities were equally juicy. They were birds of a feather. They struggled to claw their way up the corporate ladder, then they played even harder to make the trip seem worthwhile. The money, the clothes, the top-of-the-line cars—all these things were perks after years of sacrificing families, relationships, even their own personal integrity. Most never bothered to marry, knowing that work would always come first. Those who did marry invariably found themselves in divorce court. Those who managed to stay married had found partners who ignored their proclivities by frequenting department stores with unlimited credit cards and indulging in wardrobes that would clothe small countries. Few had truly successful marriages. In their elite circles, a "happy" marriage was one that advanced them into higher social positions, giving them more and more financial or political clout.

"Not Robbins? Georgi, he's married! And he's an associate. You know how Mr. Wheeler feels about that." Alex's eyebrows rose ever so slightly, though his voice remained low enough for only Georgeanna to hear.

Her lips tipped to the left by a millimeter.

"We're going to The Hideaway this weekend."

"Bad idea, Georgi. Really bad idea, darling."

Georgeanna's smile held smug satisfaction.

"Just one of the perks, Alex." She smiled seductively, then she sighed. "And certainly not the end game. Just a little … precursor."

"Watch your back," he murmured, smiling as though his stomach hadn't just plummeted to his toes. "Wheeler won't like this one bit."

2003-2010

Jackson Robbins had fallen in love with Alice long ago. High school sweethearts became college lovers. She had gotten pregnant just before graduation. In a fit of social propriety, brought on largely by Alice's heart-wrenching tears, Jackson proposed. He had been ready to break it off, having caught the eye of the counselor who had suggested law school to satisfy his ambitions. Instead they raced through a discreet wedding and settled into a relatively contented routine. The fling with the counselor had come and gone, unnoticed by his adoring wife.

Then Alice miscarried. It happened only a short month after the wedding, while Jackson was out of town on an interview. She looked pale when he rushed home from the airport. She cried in his arms until grief gave way to restless sleep. Jackson retreated to the kitchen. Taking a cold beer from the refrigerator, he leaned a hip against the countertop and sighed. The reason for the wedding was gone now, but that didn't mean he should dump his grieving wife, did it? He had always cared for Alice. Maybe they could still make it work. After all, his parents had remained married for thirty-five years, until his dad died of a heart attack a couple of years ago. His mother would be scandalized if he up and divorced his wife only weeks after the wedding.

"You haven't even tried to make it work, Jackie," she would say, her furrowed brows broadcasting disapproval.

Jackson heaved a sigh. *Maybe it wouldn't be all that bad.*

~~~~~

Alice found a job in retail. She hated every minute—customer complaints, inventory headaches, security issues, and general multi-tasking, and she never failed to let Jackson know how much she hated it. Her college degree opened the door for a mid-level management position, but even her rare days off were interrupted by frantic phone calls from both the store and the home office.

Still, Jackson was in law school. This was temporary. Once Jackson was safely established in a law firm, she'd be able to quit.

Then Jackson dropped out of law school.

"It's just not my cup of tea," he told Alice.

"I'm not supporting you so you can be a student forever, Jackson!"

"Oh, so you want to sit around eating bonbons while I support you. Is that it? Why did you even go to college, Alice?"

Alice's face lost all color.

Battle lines in the sand. But Jackson knew he needed her income to live on while he switched to finance. He apologized and seemed more appreciative—for a time.

Headhunters visited the college and Jackson worked hard to catch their attention. He accelerated his classes and excelled at every course. He'd found his niche in life.

When Jackson came home one afternoon, he swept her off her feet, and whirled her around in a circle until she begged him to stop.
~~~~~

"I got it, Alice! I think I got the position in New York! They liked my presentation—no, they *loved* my presentation!"

Alice wanted to put in her two weeks' notice immediately.

"No, babe," he said, setting her down with a thud. "Not yet. We've got three weeks to graduation, then I'll fly to New York to meet with the top guys. Just hold off until then."

"But Jackson, I'll need to pack out the apartment, and we'll have to find an apartment in New York. I should come with you."

But Jackson shook his head. "Not this trip, baby. They only gave me one ticket. If it looks like I'm in for sure, I'll look into an apartment before I come back."

"You're going to choose a place to live without me?" she said, hurt radiating from her eyes.

"What? You think I can't pick out an apartment without your expertise?" His tone vibrated with belligerence.

"I'll be the one setting up our home, Jackson. I should at least have a say in it."

"It's a New York apartment!" Jackson's temper exploded. "It's not rocket science."

The argument went downhill from there. Finally, Jackson told her to write down all the amenities she insisted their home had to have. It took her a week to compile the list, which led to another fight.

Alice insisted on decent schools, close to upscale shopping, someplace with room for cars. She would not give up her car.

"It's New York, Alice. Most people don't even try to keep cars in the city."

"I'm not going to be stuck at home while you work all the time," Alice shot back.

"They have these marvelous inventions called taxis. Or subways. Use public transportation, for-crying-out-loud!"

His sarcasm slapped her face and tears stung her eyes. "Oh, sure, what a great idea. And wind up as a statistic on a police blotter? No, thanks, Jackson. You really care about my safety."

"And why are we worried about schools, Alice? We don't have children. Remember?"

"But we could try, couldn't we? It's been three years since I lost the baby, Jackson. If you do get this job, we could think about starting a family."

"*If* you get pregnant again, we'll think about a house in a suburb," Jackson said, rolling his eyes. "The kid won't pop out ready for kindergarten, you know. We'd have a few years before we'd need to worry about that."

Alice fumed. "You're always right, aren't you, Jackson?"

Jackson sighed. Life with Alice was beginning to get on his nerves. But married men seemed to make it in the business world, and he wanted that success. Besides, his mother would never understand if he divorced Alice. Why did women always seem to stick together?

In the end, he did get the job — and he found a lovely apartment on 8th Avenue. There was even a parking garage for their cars, though Alice rarely took hers out of its assigned slot.

2010-2020

Jackson was a junior partner in one of New York's top stock market brokers. He worked eighty-to-ninety-hour weeks for them — for their future. At least that was what he told Alice every time he had to bail on a social engagement.

Alice's working days were over. This was her reward for those hard years in retail. She had a whole new circle of friends among the wives of Jackson's older associates. She had a wardrobe labeled by designers she had once sold, but had never been able to afford herself. She attended society luncheons, fund-raising dinners, and volunteered for all the socially acceptable causes.

Mrs. Wheeler was the boss' wife, and she took Alice under her wing. For the next ten years, Alice attended every office function, then every luncheon Mrs. Wheeler invited her to. She watched carefully and she learned more than she would have ever dreamed possible.

But she rarely saw Jackson.

And there were no more pregnancies.

Today

Then lightning struck. The routine rifling of pockets before the dry cleaners picked up for the week usually yielded little beyond the stray coins. When she found his day planner in the inner pocket, her anxiety rose a notch. The standing joke was that Jackson didn't use the restroom without consulting his day planner. When she found the ad for "The Hideaway" in the inside pocket of the planner, anxiety ratcheted into anger.

Jackson was supposed to be in San Francisco on business. This ad showed a bed and breakfast in upstate New York.

Her first call was Darlene Douglas, whose husband worked in Jackson's office.

"Hey, Darlene," she said, her voice tense. "Did Gary mention Jackson's trip to San Francisco this weekend?"

"Jackson's trip?" Darlene laughed. "No, Gary went to San Francisco, honey. He said he owed Jackson a favor or something. Sounds like they were betting on the Giants game again."

"Are you sure?" Alice whispered.

"Of course, I packed for him yesterday and he flew out early this morning." Darlene's voice changed slightly. "What is it, honey? Did you two fight again?"

"No, not exactly." Alice debated how much to tell Darlene. Should she be airing their dirty laundry to her friends? But it was Darlene. They were practically joined at the hip these days. "Darlene, he left his day planner behind. And he said he was going to San Francisco for the weekend." She gulped, panic rising in her voice. "And then I found this pamphlet."

"What pamphlet?" Darlene's voice was quiet.

"It's f-f-for a place called The Hideaway," Alice said, giving way to tears.

The line was quiet.

"Darlene?"

"Yeah."

"Have you heard of this place?" Alice's voice rose. Gary and Darlene had about the best marriage in the company. She could never understand how Gary made it to so many of the functions Darlene signed them up for, when Jackson hadn't even made half of their engagements. Questions of that nature erupted in fights in her own house though.

Darlene exhaled loudly. "Yeah, I've heard… rumors."

"What have you heard?" Alice's voice was low. She clutched the phone until her knuckles throbbed.

"It's … well, it's a place some people use for … trysts," Darlene said. "Gary tried to get the information so we could have a weekend away from the baby one time. He was told…"

"Told what?"

"Well, that it wasn't really appropriate for married couples. It

might be embarrassing if we ran into anyone else who might be …
there at the same time. It's something like a company perk. Anyway,
no one would give him further information, and he just let it go."

"Who told him that, Darlene?" Pieces fell into place like dominos
standing too long in formation. Silence on the other end of the
connection spoke louder than words. But the answer took her by
surprise.

Finally, Darlene answered. "I think it was Georgeanna Weston."

Alice knew Georgeanna from the office functions. She had
seemed like a nice lady, though a little cold. But she was single, so
maybe she utilized the bed and breakfast, and who could blame her?
But why did Jackson have a flyer for this place?

Alice's eyes narrowed. Someone was encroaching on her
marriage.

That was not going to happen.

Upstate New York

Alice sat up. She found herself face to face with a young man
holding a snapped ammonium carbonate capsule under her nose.
She coughed. Smelling salts.

"Easy, Ma'am," said the young man, his hand on her arm to
prevent her from bolting to her feet. "Just stay put here. You make
any sudden moves and we'll be picking you up off the floor. Lucky
for you, old Hardwood caught you before your head hit one of those
flagstones."

The young man wore an EMT's uniform with the name Sam
Wellington on the nametag. His light brown hair tickled the neck of
his shirt, and curled over his forehead in soft waves. His blue eyes
were rimmed by the thick lashes that most women had to work hard
to achieve. Bedroom eyes.

Alice frowned. "How did you know…?"

The young man smiled. "About the flagstones? That's easy. My
granddaddy owned that property for years. Inherited it from his
granddad too, but nobody's lived in it since around 1910. Some big
company bought it about forty years ago, and they spent a fortune
fixing it up. Fancy carpets and antique furniture, new roof. But they
didn't keep it up, and it sort of fell apart. Guess they didn't realize
just how much money it takes to keep a business like that up and
running."

Alice leaned back against the leather sofa cushions. She stared at the sofa in confusion.

"How did I get here?"

Sam laughed. "You scared the sheriff silly, ma'am. He's not used to dealing with damsels in distress. He carried you back to his car and hauled you back to his office with lights and sirens. Called dispatch to have me meet him here to take care of you. He swears he tore up two or three discs in his back."

Alice felt her face heat up. "I'm not that heavy," she huffed.

"No, ma'am," Sam said, "but he ain't getting any younger and he's carrying about eighty pounds too much for his age. I carried you in here for him, but he's on the cranky side now."

Carried her... Memory returned in a rush. Bloody car seats— Jackson's grey Mercedes Benz beside the bed and breakfast.

"My husband?" she asked weakly.

He nodded toward the next room where they could hear the sheriff's raised voice. "Hardwood's trying to get a search warrant, but I gather he's running into a little bit of resistance."

"But the car..." she said, shaking her head in disbelief. "He's been there at some point. He could be hurt! There was so much blood on the seat. I just don't understand. Why would he even come to such a remote spot? And where is he now?" Tears streaked her cheeks, and Sam's gaze filled with pity.

~~~~~

"Yes, sir... I do understand... No, sir... Yes, I do know how high-strung some wives can get, but I'm afraid we've got another issue... Yes, sir, I do understand about privacy, but..."

Sheriff Hardwood was accustomed to holding conversations where he held the controlling reins. But this sanctimonious little squirt wasn't letting him get a word in edgewise. The call to the judge had been forestalled by the New York corporation that owned the property. Without more cooperation from the owner of record, the judge hesitated to violate their privacy. After all, the property was posted with 'no trespassing' signs.

"Look!" Harwood's voice exploded and shocked the man on the other end of the phone. "I've got an abandoned car on your property, and I've got a missing man. That's probable cause and the law allows me to kick the damn door down if you don't want to cooperate with me. And that's precisely what I'm going to do if you don't patch me through to your boss this minute. Is that clear? Court order or no
~~~~~

court order, I **am** going to search that house. You can help me out, but if you don't, I will break down that very expensive-looking oak door. A man's life is at stake. Now I am done arguing with you. Are you putting me through to your boss or not?"

"Good," Sheriff Hardwood said after a three-second pause. "Thought you'd see things my way," he muttered under his breath. He didn't want to tell this twit about the interior of Jackson Robbins' car.

He took the phone away from his mouth briefly and called to the next room. "Sam?"

The young man patted Alice's hand awkwardly, and hollered over his shoulder. "Yeah, Sheriff?"

"How's she doing in there?"

Sam smiled at Alice and rose to his feet, indicating with one index finger that he'd be right back.

He approached the desk and lowered his voice. "I don't know, Sheriff. I'm afraid she's in shock, but I don't think she'll agree to go to the hospital. At least not 'til after you've searched that house."

The sheriff held up a finger and pulled the phone back to his mouth. "Yes, who am I talking to now? … Mr. Wheeler? Yes, sir, you own this property under my jurisdiction, and we've got a serious problem. Did your assistant explain the situation?... Uh huh… Uh huh… Then do you know this Jackson Robbins? … I see… Uh huh… Yeah, I've got Mrs. Robbins right here in my office. She may need some medical attention, but I don't think she's going to leave 'til you let us search that house. Since I don't want her camping on my office couch, I think we'd better investigate this matter and settle it once and for all… Yeah, I can wait for him… One hour? Mr. Wheeler, let me be real clear about this. If your man isn't here in an hour, I'll be going back out there without the key and you'll be replacing the door. You understand me, sir?... Yes, well, I've had all the stonewalling I'm going to take for one day, so you can thank that little squirt who answered your phone for my 'crankiness'… Yeah, well, I'm glad to hear you're going to cooperate, Mr. Wheeler. You just get that man on the road pronto."

The sheriff hung up the phone and rose to his feet. "Might need you to stick around for a bit, Sam. Think you can manage her?"

Sam looked over his shoulder toward the office. His wife would be expecting him for supper soon, but that poor lady looked so shattered.

"Sure, Sheriff. I can stick around. Just need to call Janie and tell her I'll be late."

"Good man," Sheriff Hardwood said, slapping the younger man on the shoulder hard enough to stagger him. "You've got a good wife there. You go call her and I'll talk to Mrs. Robbins for a few minutes."

Sam nodded, pulling his cell phone from his pocket and heading outside for a bit of privacy. Sheriff Hardwood took a deep breath and lumbered toward his office.

~~~~~

Sam could hear the baby crying in the background when Janie answered the phone.

"Please don't tell me you're going to be late," Janie said, trying to keep her tone light. "I made your favorite tonight. Fried pork chops, baked potatoes, and marmalade carrots."

"What's the special occasion?" he asked, trying to keep his voice equally light.

"You don't remember?" Janie's voice dropped a little bit. "It's our eighteen-month anniversary, Sam."

Eighteen months? He sighed and rubbed his forehead. *It's hard enough keeping track of the whole years. How does she expect me to keep track of the half years too?* "Well, honey, I might not make it home very early tonight. We've had sort of a situation here."

"Where are you, Sam? Please don't tell me you're at the bar with the guys tonight..." Janie bit her lip. She tried so hard not to nag, but she hadn't known that marriage to the man of her dreams would be so lonely.

"No, baby," Sam said, pleading with his voice. "Look. This lady came in from New York City to find her husband, and somehow it looks like he ended up out at the old Hideaway place."

"Why would he go to a broken-down old building, Sam?" As hard as she tried, Janie had a difficult time believing that this was more than another tall tale of Sam's. He'd always been a little bit obsessed with the old place.

"I don't know, Janie, but something went really wrong out there. The sheriff says the car was full of blood. He's having it towed in right now."

"But, Sam, you don't work with the sheriff. Why do *you* have to be late?"

"The wife," Sam said, trying to be patient, but the baby upped his game in the screaming department, and a headache had started
~~~~~

in the back of his neck. "She's … well, it's either shock or she's getting ready to have a doozy of a breakdown. Hardwood asked me to stick around and help him deal with her. She evidently passed out cold out at the house."

"You're out at the old place?" Janie asked.

"No, honey, I'm at the sheriff's office. He brought her back here and called me to come take a look at her. She should be in a hospital, if you ask me." He looked over his shoulder at the office. Mrs. Robbins might need him; he needed to get off this phone.

"Then why don't you take her to the hospital, then you can come home? Danny, stop that fussing. Momma will be there in a minute."

"Look, Janie, call Hardwood if you don't believe me!" Sam exploded. "I've gotta' get back in there. I just wanted to let you know I'll be late."

He hung up. Janie called his name twice before the line began beeping with the fast disconnect signals. She sighed. Turning to her one-year-old son, she picked him up and blinked to keep from crying right along with him. "Sh-h-h-h-h, Danny. Looks like it's just you and me again, kiddo."

~~~~~

Sam knew that marriage to one woman would be challenging. He had dated Janie all through high school, and she was always catching him with other girls. He was a hunk, after all! Sports jock supreme, and the local girls tried for four years to split them up. But there was something special about Janie that intrigued Sam. Although he had tried repeatedly, Janie had held onto her virtue until their senior year. One moment of weakness was all it took.

Janie's father had insisted on the 'come-to-Jesus' moment alone with Sam. "Son, I know you've been in love with my daughter for four solid years now. You've had your ups and downs, but she's stuck by you through everything. Even when her mother and I told her she should just let you go." Sam's eyes had popped at that. He blushed when he realized that they had probably heard more gossip about him than he'd given them credit for. "But my little girl is having a child now. Your child. Are you going to man up and marry her?"

There was only one answer you could give when a former Marine drill sergeant asked that question.

"Yes, sir."

"That's a good man," her father had said, clasping his hand.
~~~~~

"You treat her good. She deserves it."

Maybe it won't be so bad, Sam had thought glumly as he left their house that night.

The wedding had been a blast. Until Janie caught Cindy Hooper coming out of the men's room with Sam, straightening her mini-skirt and giggling. Sam fed her a line about needing toilet paper for the ladies' room, but she had turned and walked away. Then the pregnancy made its presence felt. Backaches and weariness, nausea and puking. 'Just for the first three months' turned into a nine-month marathon of misery. Janie almost lost the baby twice, and the doctor ordered her on bed rest. Sam had no trouble getting his needs met in other venues. The girls practically lined up around the block.

Now that the baby was here, he fussed far more than Sam thought was possible for any one child. *And she wonders why I go to the bar*, Sam thought as he headed back to the sheriff's office. Mrs. Robbins was an older woman, but she was still strikingly lovely. And she needed him right now far more than the little wife did.

~~~~~

Alice watched the sheriff approach. Her stomach flipped a couple of times. She'd overheard just enough of the sheriff's tirade to know that whatever he was about to tell her, it was going to change her life forever.

"Mrs. Robbins, I think we need to talk a little bit about your husband." The sheriff pulled a chair around to face her. "This firm your husband works for..."

"Market Fire," she said. "Sheriff, did you speak to them? I heard you say Mr. Wheeler's name a few minutes ago."

"Yes, ma'am, I did," he said slowly.

"Why?"

"Ma'am?"

"Why did you call my husband's boss?"

The sheriff cleared his throat. "Well, Mrs. Robbins, I didn't intend to call his employer. I was trying to reach the company who owns that old house. Just happens that the owner of record is the head of Market Fire."

Alice shook her head in confusion. "Wait a minute. My husband's company owns the property where we found his car? I don't understand."

"I don't quite understand either. But they're sending down a gentleman with the keys. Seems they got a word in with the judge to
~~~~~

keep us out, but once I got a little tougher, they decided to cooperate. We'll have to wait just a bit before going back out…"

"But, Sheriff, my husband could be hurt in that house!" Her voice rose in panic.

"Now, Mrs. Robbins, you gotta' calm down here." His hands rose toward her in a soothing motion. "Mr. Robbins has been missing for — what? Two days now? If he is in that house, ma'am, I doubt he's a case for the rescue squad. I'm sorry, ma'am, but I think you need to prepare yourself for the worst-case scenario here."

"I want to go with you —"

"No," he cut in quickly with a no-nonsense shake of his head. "No, ma'am. I don't know for sure what we're going to find, but whatever's in that house, you don't need to be there to see it. You're just going to have to trust me."

Alice covered her face and cried. Sheriff Hardwood sat quietly with the sobbing lady until Sam came back in. Then he retreated hastily to wait in the outer office for the man with the keys.

<div style="text-align:center">~~~~~</div>

Alexander Pierce got out of the car, his face pale but calm. Returning from the old house felt surreal. There was no one in the house, much to his relief. Then again, he hadn't really expected to find anyone. The sheriff had towed the gunmetal grey Mercedes to the garage, where crime scene investigators prepared to tear it apart. Blood covered the front seat, the floorboards, even the roof of the luxury car. No wonder Alice had fainted. He strode toward the one-story brick building and headed for the office where he had formally greeted Alice only forty-five minutes ago. The young EMT jumped up suddenly, jerking away from his charge. He didn't meet Alex's eyes but backed out of the way.

"Did you find…?" she began.

"No, Alice, there's no sign of Jackson."

"Who was she, Alex?"

Sam watched the exchange with a little bit of confusion. They had greeted one another formally before the foray into the old house. Now there was a familiarity between them. Sam wondered just how well they really knew one another.

"Alice…"

The front door slammed, and Alex straightened as the sheriff entered the office.

"I suppose Mr. Pierce here told you, we didn't find any sign of your husband. I'll put out a missing persons' bulletin. And I'll keep you posted, of course, but I don't know what else I'm going to be able to do. A lot will depend on the outcome of the analysis of the car.

Alex nodded in his direction and motioned to Alice. "Mrs. Robbins, I'd be glad to drive you back to the city. We can send for your car later. I'll have someone from the office take care of that for you. Right now, I don't think you need to be driving."

Sam spoke up for the first time since Alex's return. "That's a real good idea, ma'am. You shouldn't drive right now." His confused gaze slid from Alice to Alex and back again. Alice met his eyes for only a moment, then she nodded meekly. Whether or not she should drive, this was one of those moments when a wise gal just had to 'let the men-folk make the decisions.' She accepted Alex's hand and stood shakily to her feet. His arm automatically circled her waist protectively, tossing a curt nod in the sheriff's direction before escorting Alice away from the sympathetic stares.

"You have my card, Sheriff." Alex nodded one last time and they left the building.

~~~~~

Alex was uncomfortable with the grizzled old sheriff. On the few occasions when he had used the services of the Hideaway, it was plush and elegant, delightful in every way. The only time he'd seen it like this was that first time when Georgi had brought him here to explain how it worked. He thought she was trying to pull a prank on him. This type of stuff didn't happen unless Stephen King wrote it into a movie script.

"So, what is this 'monster'?" he had asked, trying to keep a straight face but failing. "Nessie, perhaps, dropping in for a quick bite? Bigfoot and his children and grandchildren?"

"It's not funny, Alex!" Georgi had jumped from the plump bed and yanked on her clothes. "This is not a joke. I'm serious."

"But why, Georgi? Why would Wheeler give us a place that turns into a monster's playground? It just doesn't make sense." He reached for her, but missed.

"How much did it cost when that little Margaret from the typing pool tried to rope you into a white picket fence and marriage license your first year here?"

Alex blushed. "I wasn't even the father," he muttered.

"I know, but we work long hours. Those who do marry, rarely see their spouses, and nine times out of ten, they wind up in divorce
~~~~~

court. This is our 'out,' Alex. I'm just saying, Mr. Wheeler doesn't want to have another fiasco like the last one. He learned a long time ago that it's just more... expeditious for a problem to disappear without a trace. He has... connections."

"To what?" Alex demanded. "A vampire? A kennel of rabid Rottweilers? The Devil?"

Georgi rushed to the bed and put her fingers over Alex' lips. "Don't joke about this, Alex. And don't say... that."

"Don't say what? The Dev..." A roar cut off the rest of his comment. The rich accoutrements of the room fell away and Alex found himself covered in cobwebs. He cursed and brushed the sticky mess from his body while Georgi shoved his pants into his hands.

"Hurry!" she whispered.

Alex squirmed into his trousers and grabbed his shirt from the floor. Georgi pushed him from the room and down the hallway to the stairwell. Wallpaper drooped in ragged layers, some blackened with scorch marks. Alex felt his eyes pop outward as he gazed at what was, only last night, an elegant entryway. He slowed as he took in the decay of decades. Another roar and a mighty vibration of a large creature's footstep spurred Georgi to shove him forward with more urgency.

"What the hell?" Alex sputtered as they fell out the door and across the overgrown flowerbed. Last night, he had admired the roses and the beds of irises and tulips. Clumps of hostas had lined one end of the property and wisteria had wound through a trellis with a bench for sitting out in the moonlight. A large shadow passed one of the upstairs windows, and Alex saw horns on a scaly head just before a flame shot out and blackened the glass.

"Was that...?" Words failed him.

"We've got to go now, Alex!" Georgi muttered, shoving him toward the car.

"But our luggage... my clothes... even my wallet."

"You really want to go back in there? Really, Alex? Be my guest."

Another roar split the air. They dove into the car.

"Hit the gas, Georgi." His voice wavered more than he liked.

"Yeah, I thought so." Georgi hit the gas and peeled down the lane to the tree-lined road, and from there to the highway toward the city.

Alex had said very little on the trip back, but Georgeanna talked nonstop, like she'd ingested crack.

"I don't understand it, though. The Dragon doesn't come out until you call it," she babbled. "You have to summon it. Once the person you want to be rid of is asleep, you slip from bed and you call on the Hideaway to summon the Dragon. He comes, you leave... problem solved. Then you tell people that you were supposed to meet at this little bed and breakfast, but couldn't get away. She's never seen again. End of story. The rest of us swear that you were in your office all weekend working on some big project. Why did it come out? I didn't call it!"

Alex got his answer on Monday morning. Mr. Wheeler summoned him to his spacious office as soon as he arrived.

"Sorry, sir. I've been trying to cancel all of my credit cards and work on the paperwork to get my company keycard replaced. Would you believe it? Got mugged over the weekend..." His voice faded away.

Mr. Wheeler held out his wallet, then pointed to his suitcase, which bore a large burn mark across the leather. "Yes, that was some 'mugging,' Mr. Pierce." His voice was sharp enough to cut ice, and twice as cold. "I want you to understand something, young man. This is not a license to do whatever you want with whomever you want. You can enjoy the Hideaway as often as you like, but the Dragon is for worst case scenarios only. We don't need a repeat of the 'Margaret disaster.' I allowed Ms. Weston to induct you into the 'club.' But you will not misuse the property. Do you understand?"

"Y-yes, sir," Alexander gulped. "So, it was you who—?"

"Called up the Dragon?" Mr. Wheeler smirked. "Yes, Mr. Pierce. I had a feeling you might need convincing. Get a good look?"

Alex paled and nodded.

"Good." He stood almost toe to toe with Alex and lowered his voice. "If you ever tell anyone what you've seen, that day will be the last day of your life. The Dragon uses the Hideaway, but he doesn't need it. He'll find you. Anywhere. Anytime. Do you understand?"

"Y-y-yes, sir," Alex murmured. "I understand completely."

He locked himself in his office after that meeting and didn't stop trembling until well after lunch time.

~~~~~

The whole time Alex and the sheriff had been in the Hideaway, he had felt the lawman's eyes on him. He shuddered to think what might happen if Hardwood ever felt that he knew more than he was telling. It had been seven years since that first encounter with the
~~~~~

Dragon, and Alex had kept expecting to hear the thumps of the monster's footfalls on the decaying floorboards. He'd been more than happy to leave the old building until it could appear to him in its splendor. Even that version held disquieting memories. Perhaps because he knew just how quickly it could revert to its decayed state.

~~~~~

Silence felt like a heavy wool blanket for the first twenty minutes of the ride back to New York City. Alex turned on the radio and a smoky voice crooned from the speakers.

> *Through a tunnel dark with trees*
> *Lies a ramshackle house of sin*
> *Devours all who venture within...*

"Who was she, Alex?" Alice asked again, turning the volume back down.

Alex sighed. "The official view appears to be that Georgeanna Helena Weston and Jackson Robbins have run away together. The car was supposed to be found in the city, not on company-owned property. That's a fact that our dear Mr. Wheeler is particularly peeved about. The blood was a set-up to make it look like someone killed your husband. In all reality, they are most likely lounging on some Caribbean beach. But you're supposed to be able to collect the life insurance. Just Jackson's little ruse to ease the guilt of deserting his wife."

"Has he deserted me, Alex? Or is he really dead?"

"Darling, I don't know. But I suspect they have left the country."

Alice sighed and ran her fingers through her long blond hair. She leaned back against the headrest. It had been a long, emotional day, and she was exhausted. Alex had been attentive at several social gatherings, escorting Alice to the dance floor while Jackson hob-knobbed with the social and political elite. And now that she thought back on the last few parties, Georgeanna had been standing closer to Jackson than she had liked at the time. As Jackson became more and more unavailable, both physically and emotionally, Alice was thrown more and more into Alex's company. He was a generous lover, romantic, gentle, and she was starved for attention. Now he was her emotional support when it appeared that her husband had deserted her. Life was certainly throwing her some curves.

"Want me to stay tonight?" Alex asked softly, taking her hand
~~~~~

in his and lifting the limp fingers to his lips.

"Is that wise?" she asked, eyes still closed.

"Probably not, but I will stay if you want me to. You don't really want to be alone tonight, do you?"

She smiled and turned her face toward his profile. "No, I want you to stay, Alex."

His smile was worth it all. Then it faded for a brief instant. "I have to report in with Wheeler," he said reluctantly, and she sighed. "I won't be long, darling, but I have to let him know how it went at the Hideaway. He'll have my head on a platter by dawn if I don't."

She turned a weary smile his way and nodded. Such was the world of Market Fire. All roads led to the mysterious Mr. Alvin Wheeler.

~~~~~

Sam sat in his car for a long time. Mrs. Robbins seemed like such a nice lady. But that little exchange between her and the New York suit left a bitter taste in his mouth. The family had always hinted at some strange things going on at the Hideaway. Sam had ventured onto the property as a kid and peeked into the windows, what few hadn't been boarded up. Some folks said that anyone who trespassed there never came back again. But he hadn't believed any of the rumors.

Until…

He swallowed hard, screams lacing his memories of Granddad's property. Something sure happened to that Robbins fellow. Sam had caught a glimpse of the car and his stomach had threatened to bring his lunch back for all the world to see. He drummed his fingers on the steering wheel of his truck. Janie was expecting him home for dinner, but he just had to poke around the old place. He knew a few hiding places that no one else was aware of—things his father had whispered on his death bed.

First, he'd drop by the bar for a drink. After a day like this one, he needed it.

~~~~~

Sam slapped a five-dollar bill on the polished bar.

"Set me up, Bobby," he said. He perched on the bar stool, hooking his heels on the lower rungs and hunching forward to rest his elbows on the edge of the bar.

"Rough day there, Sam?" the bartender asked, handing him a Budweiser.

Sam drained about half of it in one long gulp. He took a deep breath and sighed. "Yeah, guess you could say that."

"There's a rumor floating 'round about some trouble out at your Granddaddy's old place today." Bobby eyed the young man but went back to drying shot glasses.

"Yeah, some trouble…" His voice wavered a little, and he wiped a shaky hand over his face. He swallowed the rest of his beer and pushed the bottle away. Bobby shoved another bottle into his hands and waited.

"Hey, Bobby, you remember that cheerleader that used to hang all over me after the games? What was her name? Amber … something." He took a swig of the second beer.

"Yeah, Amber… uh… Johnson? No, Jenkins… Jessup. That's it. Jessup." Bobby set the shot glasses on the shelf. "What about her?"

"Well, she just sort of disappeared after high school." Sam pushed his hair back from his forehead with both hands. "You ever hear anything about her?"

Bobby laughed. "Man, you weren't the only football jock she made a play for! That gal was voted 'most likely to wind up turning tricks on a street corner.'"

"Yeah, but then she just vanished." Sam gulped down more beer.

Bobby thought about it for a few minutes. "Well, after you, then Tom Korbin…" He paused, squinting as he searched his memory. "Then there was Eric Johnson, but he moved to Boston after college. And Will Gardner, that guy who took over the gas station out on the interstate. Last I heard she took up with Andy Calhoun."

"Andy Calhoun?" Sam choked on his beer. "No kidding? He was older than both of us."

"Yeah, real shady character, from what I remember." Bobby wiped at the countertop with a wet cloth. "He had something to do with guns or something. Some outfit out of New Y--Jersey. Gang-related, I heard." Bobby had caught himself just in time. A bead of sweat trickled down his temple.

"I haven't seen him in quite a while either." Sam frowned. His eyes seemed to be focused on his beer bottle. "What ever happened to him?"

Bobby watched Sam carefully, his face blank of all expression. "Don't know, buddy. Haven't seen him. Maybe he took Amber and headed for Mexico. That guy was a couple steps away from a major arms bust. Feds showed up here about a week after he disappeared — ATF guys. Man, were they mad! He slipped right through their fingers. Guess he had the sense to get out of the country. Never saw him again."

"You ever go out to Granddad's old house?" Sam asked, looking up from his beer.

"What?" Bobby forced a laugh. "That old dump? Why on earth would I go out there? That place is ready to fall apart."

Sam shrugged. "I used to hear it was a good make-out spot."

"Yeah, right," Bobby laughed. "If you like horror movies and campfire stories."

"Dad used to tell me to stay away from the old place," Sam said softly. "He said it was… haunted… by something bad. He always said that it was dangerous."

Bobby watched Sam more closely now. "Why? You ever take girls out there?" He kept his voice light with effort.

"Once or twice," Sam whispered. He gulped the rest of his beer in one swallow, then pushed away from the bar. "Gotta get home. Janie's already irked that I had to stay at the sheriff's office so late."

"Sheriff's office! What were you doing there?" Bobby asked. But Sam was half-way out the door.

"Not good," Bobby muttered to himself as he strode to his office and punched in the New York number he kept taped to his desk drawer.

"Yeah, I think we might have a problem," he said when his call was answered. "Sam Wellington was just here asking questions… Yeah, his granddaddy… yeah, that's the one. Just thought you should know. No, sir, of course not. I know better than to say anything…. Right. Yes, sir… Yeah, he was asking about Andy Calhoun and Amber — Yes, sir, that's the one… Well, I don't know for sure, but I think he might be headed out there right now."

The line went dead. Bobby hit 'end call' and closed his eyes in regret.

"Never make deals with the Devil," he whispered to himself. But this bar was his life. Being the local eyes and ears of a powerful man — that was the price of doing business. Yeah, he'd been to the Hideaway. Once was all it had taken.

<div align="center">~~~~~</div>

Sam strode toward his pickup truck. He remembered the day he had taken Cindy Hooper out to the Hideaway. Janie was pregnant and miserable. Cindy had been available for about four months, and she was impatient for Sam to dump his wife for her. He knew the legends and gossip about the old place, but he had never done more than peek in the windows when he was a kid. Until he hit those hormone-laced teenage years.

"I have to know what's in that house," he muttered as he turned the key in the ignition and pulled out of the parking lot.

~~~~~

Janie cuddled the baby on her lap, softly singing him to sleep. Seemed like his tummy was upset most of the time these days. She stood carefully, and Danny squirmed in his sleep. She rocked him in her arms until his body went limp again. Gently, she laid him in his crib, smoothing his brow. She tiptoed from the room and returned to the kitchen to check on the food. It wouldn't do for the pork chops to be too leathery to eat. Maybe she should just put them in the refrigerator until Sam got home.

Marriage to her high school sweetheart had not been a bed of roses. She sighed. She'd loved him so much. She had taken him to church with her so many times, and he acted like he enjoyed the services at the time.

"God, did I just imagine that he had come to know You? Did I delude myself?" she groaned as she wrapped the platter of pork chops in cellophane. Yes, she had to admit to herself that she had seen just what she'd wanted to see. Her parents had tried over and over to counsel her against Sam. He was wild, a womanizer, repeatedly breaking her heart when rumors got back to her about his adventures with other girls. But he always denied the rumors, heatedly insisting that he loved her. Then when he was actually caught in his lies, he became contrite and promised it would never happen again.

But it had. So many times.

So, Janie tried to hold her family together with prayer and faith that God could turn all things to good.

A sudden wave of dizziness sent Janie reeling against the counter.

Pray.

The Voice was almost audible.

Pray.

Sam was in trouble; Janie just knew it.

"Oh Lord, wherever Sam is right now, please protect him. Please
~~~~~

bring him home safely." She stumbled into the living room and crumpled to her knees in front of the sofa. The burden to pray remained heavy, and she prayed on, focusing her whole heart on the safety of the man she loved.

~~~~~

Mr. Wheeler's gaze remained locked on Alex as he gave his report in as calm and succinct a manner as he could. It was difficult to remain calm after seeing the interior of Jackson Robbins' car. Alex swallowed hard several times, aware of Mr. Wheeler's scrutiny.

"So. What is the formidable Sheriff Hardwood planning next?" Wheeler asked.

"Let forensics do their thing on the car, then go from there. He's not being very – forthcoming – in his plans for the investigation." Alex coughed, hesitated, then finally blurted out the fears in the back of his mind. "Sir, where is Georgeanna? And Jackson?"

Wheeler stared at the young stockbroker; dark eyes bored into the young man's skull. "Purely professional interest, Alex, or... perhaps something more?"

Alex blushed, then paled. "Georgi and I were on friendly terms, sir. I'd just hate to see her come to harm, that's all. Besides, bad... things..." he swallowed hard, "... don't usually happen to our people. Just to... others."

"Georgeanna Helena Weston has caused this company enough embarrassment. Her behavior has gone beyond the acceptable limits, and she has been dealt with accordingly. No internal corporate liaisons." Wheeler's stare was rock hard. "She broke the rules. Subject. Closed."

Mr. Wheeler's eyes darkened as he observed the young executive standing nervously in front of his desk. "We serve a dark master, Alexander. You knew that when you signed on at this firm. You've accepted the perks; you've lived the high life. You know that our actions have consequences. Georgeanna chose her path. And for that matter, so did Jackson Robbins. But taking a married associate to the Hideaway? Flaunting the affair. Over the top. That property is the end game, not a play toy for her amusement. She got blood-thirsty; she enjoyed that final moment when they see the bargain for what it truly is. And Jackson went too far as well; climbed too high too fast." Mr. Wheeler's eyes never left Alex for a moment. He savored the sheen of sweat on the young man's brow, inhaled the scent of fear from his pores. With a grim smile, he continued. "I guess
~~~~~

we'll be needing a new recruit, Alexander. You'll have to sift through the talent pool at some of our preferred universities next week. Then we'll see who we can bump up the ladder to replace Georgeanna, won't we?"

Alex's pale complexion flushed as fire lit his eyes. After all, he liked Georgi, but his own progression up the ladder would proceed a little more quickly without that female barracuda standing in the way! Mr. Wheeler's next words shot the wind from his sails.

"You mentioned the charming Mrs. Robbins. Alexander, you'd best watch your back with that one, you know. Trapped her husband with a child that never existed. Yes, I know a lot more than you think I do. She plays a pretty game of being the helpless damsel in distress, but she's got a lot more inside her than you can imagine. You'd better watch yourself, young man. You won't be able to play the side games if you're going to pick up where Jackson left off. I assure you that she's more bloodthirsty than even Georgeanna, if her back is against the wall."

Alex's chin raised a hair, and his eyes flashed. *Mr. Wheeler be damned!* Alice was **not** in Georgeanna's league. Not by a long shot. A man could be happy with Alice; a man could finally settle down and be happy.

"Is that all, sir? I need to go back and check on Mrs. Robbins before I head for home," Alex said stiffly.

Wheeler nodded his dismissal and Alex strode for the door. He stopped just short of slamming the door behind him, but he fumed all the way to the elevator. How dare the old man disparage Alice's character like that! He just didn't know Alice. Alex had watched her take a backseat to Jackson's ambitions for years. Alex would show them. He'd make Alice happy.

<center>~~~~~</center>

Mr. Wheeler had seen the rebellious thoughts in Alex's eyes. *He'll be singing a very different tune if he ever tries to drag that woman to the Hideaway.* The being inside Alice Robbins was strong enough to make even the mighty Mr. Wheeler cringe. But he wondered what her next move would be.

For all his own words about not tolerating in-house liaisons, Wheeler had to face a very uncomfortable fact. He had not called the dragon this time. So, who had?

He remembered the first time he'd met the charming Mrs. Alice Robbins. The spirit inside him had cringed in her presence, and though Wheeler's carriage had remained stiffly upright, he had felt his own demons respond to her. It had been a disconcerting experience. She saw more than he ever allowed anyone to see, and her eyes seemed to scorn his exalted position in a way that no one had ever done since he had first met his father-in-law.

"Did she call you up, old friend?" he murmured to the dragon in the Hideaway. "How did she even know to do that? How did she *know?*"

Wheeler poured himself a tumbler of whiskey and downed it in a gulp. The liquor burned his throat and his eyes stung ever so briefly. He poured himself another, but sipped it this time.

"She's dangerous, that one," he murmured to the darkness beyond the windows of his penthouse office.

<div align="center">~~~~~</div>

Alice exited the shower and stood before the mirror in the bathroom. She viewed herself coldly, critically. She'd been besotted by Jackson Robbins since high school, but she'd known his interest was waning in college. One of her professors had introduced her to the art of channeling spirits from other planes. That was where she met Jezebel.

Jezebel had been a queen in her time, but she'd also been a woman who dictated her own path, her own destiny, in an era that belonged solely to men. She also housed her own personal demon and fused with it in ways that no one else had ever achieved. It was a union that had lasted well beyond the grave. She had always used sex to further her own ends, and she craved power above all else.

Alice had been like putty in Jezebel's powerful hands. Jezebel was free! Alice had gotten the marriage she wanted—to a headstrong, selfish man. It hadn't worked out as she expected it to. But Jezebel knew how to manipulate men. Alice hadn't been "Alice" in a long, long time. Her acceptance of Jezebel had gotten her further than she could have ever dreamed, and the evil being promised so much more, as long as she was allowed to steer the course. Alice agreed, Jezebel had gained a body to control. She'd manipulated Jackson when she knew his interest was waning. Marriage and a baby weren't very original, but it had worked. Tears worked too. But lately Jackson had become too enamored with the luscious Georgeanna. Threats hadn't worked. He had been all too aware of Alex's interest in his wife. Their last fight had been just before Jackson left to meet Georgeanna, and he'd laughed in her face. What could she possibly do to him? He was Wheeler's golden boy! She'd play the game his way, or he'd throw her out. Not something one said to Jezebel – in any century. But it was the laughter that had sealed Jackson's fate.

Her own social climbing had been done on Jackson's coattails. But Jezebel was tired of him. Alex Pierce would take her higher than Jackson had ever dreamed. And he wouldn't betray her. She'd make sure of that. He'd never even suspect her romp on the sheriff's sofa with that nice EMT. After all, waiting for the sheriff's return had been a boring interlude in her day. That young man had been a pleasant diversion.

And Georgeanna Weston? Jezebel detested competitors. Wheeler would just have to get himself another girl. Georgeanna had encroached on Jezebel's territory and that was unacceptable. The blood in the car would prove to be Jackson's and Georgeanna would be a wanted woman. But they would never find what was left of her. Not if the Hideaway had done its job correctly.

Oh, yes, Jezebel knew all about the Hideaway. She had learned of the old inn years ago when Jackson took his first conquest, a secretary from a prominent law firm. The call to Darlene would leave an impression, and word would eventually get out. It had been a good ruse to keep up appearances as the betrayed and bewildered little wife. Now she could groom Alex to be her partner in life—and eventually in business. Wheeler's time was running out, and she intended to make sure Alex would one day take over Market Fire. And she'd be by his side where she belonged. Maybe she'd arrange to take Wheeler to the Hideaway herself. She smiled. Oh yes, what a perfect end to his reign over the corporate giant his father-in-law had built!

For now, Jezebel donned a filmy peignoir of black chiffon and awaited Alex's return.

"I'm still the distraught widow," Jezebel reminded her reflection with a grim smile. "Mustn't look too eager."

~~~~~

Carter Morland entered the bar.

"Say, what's wrong with Sam Wellington?" he asked, plunking his cap on the bar and sliding onto a stool.

"Nothing that I know of," Bobby responded. "Why?" His heart skipped a beat.

"Looked like he'd seen a ghost. Peeled out of the parking lot like
~~~~~

his tail was on fire," Carter said. "Gimme a Sam Addams."

Bobby grabbed a bottle from the shelf and tried to appear casual. "Probably headed home to Janie. He was in the doghouse for being late tonight."

"Well, he's sure headed the wrong way for that." He chuckled. "Looked to me like he was headed out to his granddad's place. Hey! What's this?"

Bobby looked down. The Budweiser in his hand seemed to stare at him accusingly. "Oh, sorry 'bout that, Carter." He reached into the under-counter fridge and grabbed the correct beer this time.

"I'll take that one since you opened it, Bobby." John Eldritch hitched himself up on the stool next to Carter. He took a swig of the Budweiser. "Hey, what was all that stuff about the old place? Couldn't help overhearing Sam talking about the inn when he was in here. Something happen out there today?"

Jimmy Krogerman bellied up to the bar. "Yeah, the sheriff spent most of the afternoon out there. Saw him come back into town towing a fancy car of some sort. Something sort of shady must have happened. Anybody know what?"

"Wouldn't surprise me at all," John said. "That old place shoulda' been torn down long time ago. It's just a breath away from a lawsuit, if you ask me. Some kid'll get hurt poking around out there and it's all gonna hit the fan."

"Hey, Bobby, you okay?" asked Jimmy.

"Yeah," Bobby muttered. "Just ate something for lunch that disagreed with me. You guys okay here for a minute?"

"Sure, take your time," Carter said.

As Bobby headed to his office, he heard a couple of murmured comments met by guffaws and knew he was the butt of their jokes. But he didn't care. What if something did happen to Sam out there? What if Sheriff Hardwood came out to question him? What if he just happened to check Bobby's phone records? Didn't cops do that when foul play was suspected? He could be in big trouble. He had to cover his bases. He sat down, his knee jiggling nervously. He'd just have to be a 'concerned citizen,' worried about the welfare of one of his customers. Yeah, that might work.

~~~~~

Sheriff Hardwood sat at his desk and labored over the report on the day's events. His time was usually spent in far more peaceful ways than looking for bodies and examining bloody cars. The radio
~~~~~

picked up a contemporary station.

> **Through a tunnel dark with trees**
> **Lies a ramshackle house of sin**
> **Devours all who venture within…**

The phone rang and the sheriff dialed down the volume.

"Yeah, Bobby… Out to the Hideaway? Are you sure? Sam knows better than to poke around that old place, especially by himself…. Asking questions, huh? …. Well, thanks for the heads up, Bobby. How long since he left the bar… That long? … Okay, I'll wander out there and check for his truck."

The sheriff hung up the phone and leaned back in his chair. *Rough day and now an even tougher night,* he thought.

Sam was a good kid, but he had a wandering eye, if the local gossip could be trusted. And the sheriff could have sworn that he saw Sam adjusting his belt buckle when he and Alex Pierce came in from the Hideaway earlier. Him and that pretty Alice Robbins? Sheriff Hardwood had dismissed it as his overactive imagination at the time, but now he wondered. He turned the radio back up. He'd finish his report, then swing out by the old place, though he didn't relish the drive out there after dark.

> **Through a tunnel dark with trees**
> **Lies a ramshackle house of sin**
> **Devours all who venture within…**

That song had been playing when he drove out to the Hideaway with Alice Robbins. He listened to the words — really listened for the first time. It could have been written with the Hideaway in mind! After all, he'd heard the rumors all his life.

A chill ran up the sheriff's spine.

~~~~~

Sam pulled up beside the old house, silent and foreboding in the dim light of sunset. He felt a chill creep up his spine. Maybe he should just go home to Janie. A small ache started between his shoulder blades. He'd loved Janie, been infatuated with her all through high school. But he hadn't known what marriage would be like. It seemed like she complained all the time — about the house, his job, his schedule, bills, the neighbors, even his momma.
~~~~~

Nothing will ever suit her. Sam's thoughts felt glum and dark. He felt trapped in a marriage by a baby that he hadn't truly wanted. He had hoped to go to college on a sports scholarship. Fatherhood had killed all of his dreams. Janie's father expected him to "man up and take responsibility," even if that meant lowering his own goals for his future. Sam didn't realize that Janie craved adult conversation after dealing with a fussy baby all day. He never thought to ask her what she wanted out of life, what dreams she had cherished as she grew up. He never wondered what she wanted from life. He simply felt the bitterness of having a second-rate life thrust upon him.

When Sam had the fling with Charlene Carson, it was a one-night stand—a few too many drinks at the SwayBack. But of course, she seemed to think there would be other opportunities in her future. That was the first time. Then there was Milly Burnside—definitely more than a one-night stand, until she found out that Sam wasn't going to leave his wife. But Cindy Hooper was the worst. It had started in the restroom at the wedding reception, and continued as Janie's pregnancy remained difficult. She had threatened to tell Janie all about their affair. That was the last time Sam had taken a girl out to the Hideaway.

Then today with Alice Robbins… Sam never expected her to fall into his arms. She had seduced *him*. That was a first in his checkered history. He hoped the good sheriff never hit that couch with luminol and infrared light!

Sam sighed and stepped out of his truck. The house crouched like a silent monster in the overgrown weeds. What did it really hold? Was Jackson Robbins' body still in there, in one of the many hidden alcoves he'd heard about as a child? He should have just told Sheriff Hardwood about the secret doors and panels in the old house, the ones his dad had told him about. He could have explored with the crew he took out there.

The house seemed to call to Sam.

He'd always managed to cajole women into coming out to the property with him on some pretext, usually as a challenge about their fear of ghosts. But the girls were never seen again. With the first two, he had pushed them in the front door, then slammed and locked it behind them. Then he retreated to the road until they stopped screaming. But the last time was the worst.

He couldn't leave Janie. Her dad would break him into little pieces with his bare hands if he broke her heart. Sam saw how Cindy acted in public, and he knew she was incapable of being discreet. It was time to end the whole thing, especially when she threatened to tell Janie. He talked up the haunted house stuff he'd heard all his life, all the little stories and rumors. Cindy had laughed at all of it. Once they stopped on the porch, he had turned to her and demanded that she leave him alone. It had to end. He was married to Janie, and that was that.

"You'll be sorry, Sam," she said, her face twisted into an angry sneer.

Lord, how could I have ever thought she was worth the trouble? he had thought with disgust. Then he gave her a push over the threshold into the entryway, slamming the old door behind him.

Let her figure out how to get out of there if she can.

Then he had felt the impact tremors on the floorboards of the porch. He had paled and stumbled backward. There had been a roar that rattled the windows, then Cindy had screamed.

"Saaaaaaaaaaaaaaaaammmm! Help me! Oh, God, no…. Saaaaaaaaaaam! Saaaa—" Her voice cut off. Fire flashed against the window panes, then silence.

Cindy was never seen again.

Sam still didn't know for sure what had happened to the girls he left in that old house. After Cindy, he had never gone out there again. The screams still haunted him.

He couldn't bring himself to approach the front porch, so he circled the building to the back door. The steps creaked and shifted under his weight, but the rickety wood beneath him held. The entry was overgrown with ivy and few knew it even existed. The padlock was old and rusted, but Granddad's key still worked. He pushed open the door and stepped inside, shining a high beam flashlight around the kitchen. Rats skittered in the corners and the flutter of birds' wings rustled high in the upper floors. Nests in the attic, probably. Or bats. He took another step toward an old pantry door and shivered. His granddad had told him about the secret panel beneath the lower shelf.

Suddenly the back door swung shut with a sharp bang. Sam whirled around and lunged for the old brass knob. Tugging did nothing. It remained sealed shut. Sam turned back to the interior of the house, his breath coming in ragged gasps. Something moved in the darkness, the vibrations trembling through the floorboards into the soles of his heavy boots. Sam swung the flashlight in the direction of the noise. He raced toward the front of the house, dodging ghostly lumps of furniture beneath drop cloths. He grasped the ornate knob on the heavy oak door. He twisted, but the door held fast. Then suddenly, the knob burned red hot, and Sam yelped as he shook his hand. What had turned the knob into molten lava? Training the flashlight on his hand, he stared at the blackened flesh of his palm; blisters red and swollen rimmed the burn.

Heavy footfalls echoed down the staircase and sulphureous fumes filled the air. Sam turned slowly, his heart pounding hard enough to crack ribs. Golden eyes flashed in the glare of the flashlight, and Sam screamed in the face of the horned creature, its iridescent scales casting glittery shimmers against the peeling wallpaper of the foyer. The neck stretched upward as it roared its displeasure at the strong beam in its eyes. Flames scorched the ceiling and the ornate chandelier shook as the chains melted and it crashed to the floor at Sam's feet. Wind whistled down the stairs behind the monster, blowing back Sam's hair and tugging at his clothes. The golden eyes focused on Sam's quaking body.

A dragon? Here? **Why? How?**

The dragon tilted its head as though it recognized Sam, knew his thoughts, maybe remembered the meals it had enjoyed at the end of Sam's affairs.

"So this is what they saw…" he whispered hoarsely.

Now he knew. But he would never get a chance to warn anyone else about the Hideaway. He'd never see his son or Janie again. In that final moment, he regretted all that he'd done, regretted not trying harder to make Janie happy.

"God, I'm sorry!" he screamed. "What have I done, God? What have I done to my family? Jesus, forgive me!"

The dragon reared back. It roared in agitation. It huffed as if to expel flames, but nothing happened. The dragon raised its head high and roared again. Rage flared in its eyes, and it tried once again to approach Sam.

Sam fell to his knees. Words from the sermons he'd heard endlessly but not paid heed to echoed in his head and he pleaded with God to take care of the family he had so neglected. He felt hot breath on his neck and knew his number was up.

Then… silence.

Sam opened his eyes and glanced cautiously around the room.

Empty.

Scrambling to his feet, Sam raced for the back door. This time it opened, and he tore out of the house. He threw himself into the truck and slammed it into gear, still cradling his blistered right hand close to his chest.

Have to get home to Janie. Have to get home to my family.

~~~~~

Janie bandaged Sam's hand carefully while he babbled. All of it came out. The affairs, the lies. Even the dragon. Then Sam was on his knees, clinging to Janie's waist.

"I'm so sorry, Janie. I'll never do it again. I promise." His voice broke into sobs. "God saved me today, Janie. He wouldn't do that if I was beyond redemption, would He? Can you ever forgive me?"

Janie stroked his hair absently. Her thoughts were still on the insistent demand that she had had to pray. She'd been on her knees for over an hour, and her husband had been miraculously delivered from death, according to his account. But he had also engineered the disappearance of three women, if his tale was to be believed. What was she going to do with that? How would she ever be able to trust him again?

"We need to call Reverend Parker," she said softly.

"No! Please don't make me confess this to him, baby, please..." Sam cringed.

"Do you really want to be forgiven, Sam? Or is this just another tall story to make me feel sorry for you?" Janie asked. Her voice was soft, but the tone held steel. "If you're serious about turning your life around, there have to be some amends made here. By your own admission, you took three women out to that house and left them. They were never seen again. Do you think we can just walk away from that? If you truly repent of your sins, you have to accept the consequences, Sam."

"But what if they lock me up?" Sam wailed. "I'll lose you and Danny."

"You'll lose us anyway, Sam. If you just claimed you repented to get yourself out of a tight fix, without meaning to change your ways, sin will just reach out and snare you again. I can't live with that, Sam. If you're serious about getting right with God, I'll stand by you. But I have to see some action to back up that kind of support. What you've admitted to me is so disgusting, so hurtful, I can't breathe. You've betrayed me in the worst ways a husband can betray his wife. You've betrayed your son by your lifestyle and your lies."
~~~~~

She pulled away from him and leaned against the countertop with her back to him.

"I can't live like this anymore, Sam. I can't live with a man who has trampled his wedding vows in the dirt like you have. Maybe we should just call it quits. I'll take Danny and go to my parents —"

"No!" Sam cried. "Don't leave me, Janie. Please!"

Danny cried, his wails interrupting them. Janie moved slowly toward the nursery, her movements slow and labored. Sam remained slumped on the kitchen floor. When she came back carrying Danny, he still knelt on the floor.

"Okay," he whispered.

"Okay?" she echoed.

"Call the preacher."

Janie froze. He looked up and saw her eyes, red and swollen. She'd been crying as she had changed Danny's diaper and calmed his tears. Standing there with his son in her arms, she had never looked more beautiful. Sam knew he'd do anything to keep this woman in his life. She had been here praying. She'd told him. She'd known he was in trouble, and even after the terrible way he'd treated her, she had prayed for him. If she insisted he had to walk over hot coals, he'd do it. Janie might be the only reason he wasn't dragon chow right now.

~~~~~

Reverend Parker was still in the living room with Sam. Janie looked at the digital clock on the stove. 12:45. She bounced Danny while he chewed on his fist and cried. The microwave dinged and she removed the bottle of formula, shook it vigorously, then tested it on her wrist. When he was guzzling it down, his little cheeks pumping down the warm liquid, she sat in one of the kitchen chairs and leaned back. Exhaustion was taking its toll.

"Our marriage is broken into a thousand pieces, Lord," she whispered, cradling her child in her arms as he succumbed to the warmth of a full belly. "How can we ever pick up all the pieces? It doesn't feel like there's any hope of going back to any semblance of normal life."

Then let Me create something new.

Sam had already broached the idea of renewing their vows. He promised that this time, he'd mean every word, and he wouldn't take anything in those vows for granted. Reverend Parker seemed to think it was a good idea.
~~~~~

She shook her head with a mirthless laugh. "Something new? Out of a mess like this? I can't do it this time, God. I've been turning a blind eye for too long, and I just can't do it anymore."

I can do all things through Christ who strengthens me.

"He betrayed me, Lord. Over and over and over… I can't forgive this kind of betrayal. I can't love him after hearing all that he's done."

Judas betrayed me, yet I loved him. I had called him to follow me and for three years, he did. He was among My closest friends. Peter denied Me. I gave him the honor of building my church. Janie, just follow Me.

"I can't trust him, Lord. How can I live with a man I can't trust?"

Trust Me.

She paused. All the years of sitting in church, reading her Bible, praying, believing. She had listened as Sam repeated the sinner's prayer with Reverend Parker. His confession appeared heartfelt. His whole demeanor had changed over the last three hours.

Could God really do something new in their marriage? Could He change Sam's heart? If she didn't believe those things, could she even call herself a Christian? Ouch. That one hurt.

Trust Me.

She remembered the way Sam had stumbled through the door. His hand had been swollen and blistered. She had cleansed it gently while he blubbered his confession, spread burn ointment from his own kit when she would have gladly ground salt into the wounds instead, then bandaged it as gently as she cared for Danny. She had loved this man once. Or maybe she had loved who she thought he was. Maybe it was time they both took another look at each other and learned to love from a new place, a place of forgiveness, a place of open eyes and more realistic expectations. He would work unpredictable hours, but if he could keep from cheating on her…

Maybe?

Trust Me.

She'd been a believer since she was twelve years old. Did she really trust God? Did she believe His promises? Hadn't He delivered her husband today?

Trust <u>Me.</u>

They still had to weather a visit with the sheriff, an investigation into the whereabouts of the three women Sam had taken to the Hideaway, and possibly a scandal big enough to knock the World Series off the front page of the newspaper. To say nothing of the repercussions when her father found out about Sam's confession! If Daddy let Sam live through the year, it would truly be a miracle.

Trust Me.

"I do," she whispered.

Somewhere in the night, a beast roared. Janie heard it. Sam cried out in the next room. He had heard it too. Reverend Parker's voice rose as he prayed for the enemy to be bound from hurting Sam or Janie. He prayed for divine protection over them, over their household. He loosed a heavenly war against the powers of darkness as Sam's 'amens' rang with more and more conviction.

"You lost this one," Janie whispered. "And you can't have him back."

The anguished shriek pierced the night one more time, then fell silent.

End

JAX
By Michelle L. Levigne

*Set in the AFV DEFENDER universe, near the end of **Here There Were Dragons**.*

Confri Audascus held her breath as the science vessel *Perelandra* slid into the Chute leading from Draxonis to Castitarus. She kept her eyes open and tried to relax completely into the support of her chair in the Gate studies lab. Other than a few flickers of prismatic shifting at the edges of her vision, she had almost no indications that the ship had entered a Chute. No warping of sensory information as her physical body tried to interpret waves in a dimension not normally inhabited by Human.

"We just hit the mother lode," Tech Cullin announced from his monitoring station on the other side of the lab.

"Tease," Confri murmured.

He gave her his approximation of an evil chuckle and for the next four minutes, as the ship traversed the Chute, he tapped controls and studied the data scrolling across five screens in front of him. A chime shimmered through the ship as the *Perelandra* emerged from the Chute. A subliminal chime echoed it, deep inside Confri's head. A deep purple light flashed across her optic nerves and a tickle of energy blipped from the bio-link implanted in the base of her skull and the protective membrane cushioning her brain. There was a subliminal click as the bio-link that linked her brain with the ship's systems disengaged.

Confri exhaled and closed her eyes and slumped for a few heartbeats. Then she took another deep breath, gripped the armrests of her chair, and lurched to her feet.

"Anything bad?" she said, as she crossed the lab to stand behind Cullin. He played his control panel like another man would ply a basso-profundo, thirty-octave wind organ.

"Heh, since when do you want the bad news first?" He tipped his head back to look at her upside down.

"Since I'm hoping there isn't any, because I've got a family reunion ahead of me and I don't want to spend my first five hours in orbit being scanned and running thirty levels of analyses."

"Family reunion?"

"One of my brothers is chief engineer on the *Defender*." She refused to mention Finn, who had been ambushed by the typical Maniterri selfish, self-righteous stupidity. For all she knew, her incoming ship had passed the ship evacuating Finn and other victims of the Castitaran illness, bescere, through the Chute to the nearest medical station.

"Is he the one who's as hyper-sensitive to energy sheets as you are?"

"No, that was Acon. Past tense." Confri sighed. "So, any sign of damage on my part?"

Her bio-link was classed as "permanent experimental phase," constantly being upgraded. Confri's sensitivity to energy fluctuations and her ability to physically manipulate some energy pulses had R&D teams throughout the Fleet and Alliance waging political wars to commandeer her time. Top priority, after solving the cocoon and Hiver problem, was refining Human-computer interface technology. She would likely never be assigned to one specific ship, and that suited her. She liked to be on the move, exploring, experimenting, seeing just what new dimensions of energy and knowledge she could open up next.

Her Talent hadn't been considered completely unique until her foster-brother, Acon, who had the same Talent, had been injured during a test run of new ship-borne technology two years ago. The emotional and psionic damage was as crippling as the physical. He was still recovering, and the general consensus was that his hyper-sensitivity to energy fluctuations would never return.

Cullin ran through the data from the medical monitors that had watched over Confri's physical reactions to the short transition through the Chute. She breathed a silent prayer of thanks to Enlo that nothing had flared or revealed the slightest flicker of negative reaction. Though her magnified sensitivity helped her detect depths and variations and new frequencies before sensors could, she was more resistant to the negative effects of the sensory warping inherent in traveling through a Chute. Still, there was always a chance that the newest Chute to be discovered and analyzed would generate a negative reaction. An allergic reaction, in the parlance of the doctor currently charged with keeping Confri in top physical condition, so she could implement her unique Talent studying this newly discovered, heretofore only theorized Chute.

With that question settled, they got to work analyzing what Confri's bio-link had revealed. They anticipated being stationed here for a long, long time. A time-lock Chute had been nothing but fable and legend, until the *Defender*'s Gate team and her genius inventor engineer brother, Jasper Lore, had come up with the technology to detect it being "born."

Confri looked forward to days with Jasper and his legend-generating team on the *Defender*, tossing ideas back and forth and comparing data. She also looked forward to seeing Treinna, Jasper's wife, and their daughter, Tress, whom she hadn't seen since the little girl was six. Very few of the derelict ship foster-siblings had settled down enough to find husbands or wives. So far, Jasper was the only one to have a child. Acon would have been next, and had established a psionic bond with his sweetheart. Then Hivers attacked the ship they were on. Confri firmly believed the snapping of the fledgling bond had crippled Acon's Talent, as well as breaking the sibling bond between him and her.

Cullin and Confri had assembled a general overview of the data, promising to open new dimensions of understanding of Chutes, by the time Captain Minerbec contacted them. Time for the briefing before the *Perelandra* settled into paired orbit with the *Defender*, around Castitarus.

~~~~~

Three hours later, Confri was still slightly in shock over the information included in the briefing. It was a good kind of shock, and she supposed she would find it amusing in a few hours. Especially after she got together with Jasper and his family, and got their perspective on what the *Defender*'s crew had been going through.

A general understanding of the situation involving the *Dandridge* and the disgraced Maniterri ambassadorial party was given to the crews of the ships sent to take over for the *Defender*. The revelation that the legends of the Castitaran dragons, numenjax, were based in fact was new, and being kept as quiet as possible. Even more surprising, the numenjax were alive. They had made contact with the two strongest psionic Talents on the *Defender*. Until the climate of Castitarus returned to its normal cycles, they were staying underground and establishing communication through strong psionic Talents.
~~~~~

Confri had been worried, when she learned that the dracs discovered on Draxonis, on the other end of the Chute the *Perelandra* had just traversed, were genetically engineered, miniaturized versions of the numenjax. Her sister-in-law, Treinna, had been "adopted" by a drac. Confri worried that Treinna, and the other drac "parents" on the Defender, would be basically conscripted to serve as communication channels for the numenjax, because they already had that psionic bond. Granted, Treinna was the chief communications officer on the *Defender*, but serving as mouthpiece for a dragon wasn't exactly part of the expected job description. Suddenly, Confri wasn't as excited about meeting a drac as she had been just a day ago.

The other information about Castitarus and what the ship's sensors had picked up when entering this solar system was fascinating but paled against those major concerns. Confri listened and made notes and put aside her questions for later. She was relieved when the briefing ended, freeing her to gather up her gear and hurry to the shuttle to go to the *Defender*. Time to enjoy her day of off-duty time with her family.

One thing she didn't expect, when she stepped through the portal of the bio-signs scanner and decontamination field of the shuttle disembarkation area, was to see a dragon suddenly appear within arm's reach of her. Confri knew it was a drac, but her mind shouted, "miniature dragon." Pale green with swirls of cream, it hovered at eye level. She stopped short and Medic Shroom nearly ran into her heels before he caught himself.

"Moonrise," Treinna Lore scolded, effectively snapping Confri's gaze free of the little drac.

It let out what certainly sounded like an apologetic cheep, then vanished. Confri shook her head, then smiled in relief at the pale-haired, willowy woman standing a few meters away, with a thin, silver-eyed, grinning little girl at her side. The drac, Moonrise, popped in, above Treinna's head, and settled down to land on her shoulder.

Confri muttered an apology to Shroom and the others, whose progress she was blocking, and hurried to cross the deck. In another moment, she and Treinna were hugging. The drac hovered overhead, watching them until Confri stepped back.

"Tress ... you've gotten so big." She opened her arms, then hesitated. Could she really expect the little girl to remember her? More than three years was a third of her entire life. To her delight,

Tress flung her arms around her and smiled wider.

"Jasper wanted to be here, but ..." Treinna shrugged.

"I know exactly what he's like. I'd be worried something was wrong if he *was* here." Confri linked arms with Treinna and let her sister-in-law guide her out of the disembarkation area. Soon the three were trotting down the corridor. "Did he ever find out that we had several bets on whether he would be late for your wedding, and by how much time?"

"Was Daddy always that way?" Tress asked. She didn't sound surprised or dismayed. If anything, the little girl sounded amused.

"Unfortunately, your father has always been easily distracted. It just shows how much he loves us, that we're a lot more important to him than his engines," Treinna said.

"Are you going to join the crew, Aunt Conni?"

"No, sorry." Confri caught her breath, delighted with how easily the little girl called her aunt, after such a long absence. "My mission is to study the time-lock Chute and figure out if we can keep it open. Now that the Alliance has made friends with Castitarus, we want to make sure we help the people as much as we can. As long as we can."

"Will you get to talk to the numenjax?"

"I don't know. I guess it all depends on --"

A silver blur popped into the air in front of Confri's nose, so close she felt the brush of leathery wings and the burst of air. Then the silver figure spun through the air, screeching and weaving circles around her head. She instinctively went to her knees and put up her arms to shield her head. The silver blurring followed her.

"Granny! Stop that! Right now! Moonrise, get M'kar!" Treinna leaned over Confri, shielding her.

The name seemed to be a trigger, eliciting more angry chattering and rasping from the silver flying menace. It darted up to the ceiling and hovered, its wings fluttering fast enough to be a blur. Confri dared to lower her arms and look. Her attacker was a little silver drac with red and yellow spinning eyes. Their gazes met, the creature let out one harsh, rasping shriek, and popped out of sight.

"Granny was really mad," Tress whispered. The whole attack didn't take more than two minutes at the most.

"What did I do to set her off?" Confri asked.

"There's no telling. She's been snapping circuits ever since the numenjax refused to bow in submission." Treinna stood up and held out a hand to help Confri get up.

Moonrise popped back in and crooned as she settled on Treinna's shoulder. An access panel farther down the corridor slid open and a dark-haired woman leaped out, hit the deck running, and hurtled toward them. She slowed after only a dozen steps. A brown drac popped into the air over her head.

"Are you all right?" she asked as she caught up with them.

"Granny went nuclear on Aunt Conni," Tress announced.

That earned a snort and a crooked grin from the woman. Then Confri saw the blue tattoo lines extending the woman's eyebrows, the gold lightning bolt and red arrow by her temple. This was Lt. M'kar, Chief of Talents, Nisandrian, and in charge of helping her acclimate to Castitarus. Confri's psionic Talent was just unique enough for some concern whether she would encounter trouble, being within psionic broadcast range of the numenjax.

"If the dracs don't like me," she said, thinking aloud, "then maybe the numenjax won't let me stay near the planet?"

"Granny is in continual hissy mode. Her opinion doesn't matter." M'kar's grin widened. "What do you want to bet there's something special about you, loud enough to irritate her?" She tipped her head to meet the gaze of the brown drac that perched on her shoulder. "What do you think, Barroo?"

He crooned and bobbed his head, and his eyes sparkled blue and green. That must have been good, because Tress laughed and Treinna smiled, and Moonrise joined in with happy chirps.

~~~~~

Confri spent a pleasant family evening with Jasper, Treinna and Tress. She was pleased when Moonrise accepted petting and treats, and crooned and trilled happily during the process.

The next day was busy. There was so much information to gather, to assimilate, and to discuss with various members of the crew. Even before her off-duty day ended, she got to work conferring with Loryn Speranzi, possessor of the latest version of the bio-link. Before Confri and Cullin could get to work on investigating the Chute, she needed to access the *Defender*'s systems and all the sensor readings it gathered while traversing the Chute, and all the readings since coming into orbit around Castitarus.

When Confri met with M'kar, she was momentarily surprised to have a third person participate in the preliminary testing of her Talent. Then she learned that the young man in a hoverchair was Thyal, a Le'ankan master. Not just a Le'ankan master, but son of
~~~~~

Premier Master Reydon. She was intrigued when they explained that through an incident they didn't have time to discuss or explain in any detail, the mind-circle established when they were students at the Academy had been "locked" open between them, expanding their psionic abilities. Thyal would be part of assessing Confri's Talent and whether her unique psionic condition would be threatened by the proximity to the numenjax.

She nearly laughed aloud at the word "proximity," because the *Defender* was in high orbit around Castitarus. Then Thyal explained how the numenjax were a group mind, which increased the reach, power, and overwhelming volume of any contact with them. He and M'kar had been able to survive contact with the numenjax through their joined minds.

"Survive meaning exhausted, requiring healing trances and boosters of vitamins and minerals and electrolytes at regular intervals," M'kar added.

"We're concerned that some residue of the mind-link you had with your sibling might leave you more vulnerable to the numenjax mind-touch," Thyal added.

Confri nodded that she understood. She had learned not to show the pain she felt at mention of Acon and the unity they had known years ago, but the ache still throbbed through her for a few moments. Still, she was able to answer Thyal and M'kar's questions, and was grateful for their sensitivity and concern for her pain. Of course, they understood what it was like to be linked psionically with someone.

Out of all the derelict ship children, she and Acon were most likely to be genetic siblings. Portions of their genetic code were similar enough to be considered siblings or cousins. Their Talent was nearly identical, sensing energy waves, gravitational waves, and stellar phenomena without the aid of sensor equipment. Their psionic link depended on the gravitational waves and energy pulses that constantly brushed against their awareness. That link had faded slightly when Acon fell in love and developed a psionic link with Merielle, but it was still strong enough for Confri to feel his fury and terror when Hivers attacked the ship. She sounded the alarm. Fortunately, Acon's ship was in the same solar system, and Confri's captain didn't doubt her or hesitate to send help. Confri was knocked unconscious for two days, when her psionic link with Acon broke. Against all odds, the rescue team arrived in time to attack the Hiver ship and cause it to retreat without its cocooned victims. Acon hadn't been cocooned. The scientists involved theorized that his Talent projected a frequency that made him either invisible or unappetizing to the Hivers, and they left him alone. When his sweetheart was cocooned, he was nearly pulled into her deep coma, and fighting to break free damaged his psionic Talent.

Acon was now on Anwesta Medical Station. He was given medical leave for the trauma, and spent all his time looking after the cocoons of his sweetheart and the rest of her crew. The doctors trying to free the victims of their cocoons discovered he had some sort of bond with Merielle, despite her deep coma. Acon was part of the effort to make mental contact with the victims in their cocoons. He had sent a message to Confri shortly after the dracs came to Anwesta, expressing some hope for Merielle's release.

"Jasper didn't mention your brother was on Anwesta," M'kar said.

"Knowing Jasper, he probably doesn't know. Acon really didn't keep in contact with anyone after ..." Confri shrugged. "Is there really hope the dracs will get through and wake the sleepers?"

"It's too early to tell," Thyal said.

Confri tried not to let that response discourage her. She knew all too well, from what her siblings who had gone into medical work had told her, "Too early to tell" was a polite way of saying they had no idea, and perhaps no hope.

Besides, Granny was the leader of the dracs on Anwesta, and she was increasingly temperamental. Was the future really resting in the paws of these creatures?

Confri's hopes rose a little in the days that followed, as she got to know the *Defender*'s dracs. Granny was the exception, not the rule. The seven young dracs assigned to the crew charmed her. Granny's vicious looks and snarls and the standoffishness of the twelve older dracs on the ship, referred to as the teacher dracs, discouraged her. After her first and only attempt to be presented to the numenjax, Confri only felt more confused by Granny's attitude.

M'kar, Thyal and Confri had to essentially sneak into the shuttle bay to take an unscheduled trip down to Castitarus. Every time someone officially scheduled a shuttle to the planet, Granny or one of her minions showed up, to either glare balefully or mournfully at whoever boarded the shuttle. Captain Arroyan was the only other one who knew about this particular trip before they took it. She was also a drac parent, and her black Battleaxe shielded her from drac eavesdropping. For good measure, M'kar and Thyal made their dracs, Barroo and Infrenx, stay behind until the last minute, so Granny and her spying dracs wouldn't be able to guess what was up.

It didn't work very long. The moment Hanni, a shuttle pilot climbed into the shuttle and saw M'kar, Thyal and Confri waiting, and they told her their destination, security essentially went out the airlock.

Granny popped in just as the shuttle passed out of the ship. She hit the deck close by Confri's feet with enough force, she honestly expected to see a dent in it. The only mind she had ever communicated with was Acon's. Despite that, she clearly understood the fury Granny directed toward her. Somehow, she had done something that enraged the silver drac.

Enough!

A chorus of voices filling five octaves chimed through Confri's head. Through her flesh, her blood, her bones, through that multi-layered psionic web that let her track energy fluctuations and sheets and pulses.

Granny's eyes flashed from red sparkles of fury to green and yellow terror. Then she seemed to shrivel up a little. Her shrieking tirade ended on a squeak. Then she popped out as quickly as she had popped in.

"If she hasn't burned out most of her circuits with that," M'kar whispered. She whistled instead of finishing the thought. "I really need to interrogate her to figure out why she doesn't want you going down there. Maybe she thinks you'll get the numenjax to ... What's wrong?"

"Overload," Thyal said, stretching out a hand to Confri.

She realized two things.

First, the multiple voices were still chiming through her mind and body, fraying the tenuous connection between the universe and her soul. Second, everything had gone crooked around her.

No, correction -- she had gone crooked. She slid sideways and out of her seat, with a boneless sensation that would have made her laugh any other time. Maybe later?

Colors swirled around and through her. Colors she had never seen before and couldn't even begin to give a name to, because they couldn't compare to anything. The colors had smells. Some of them weren't particularly nice. Especially the smells that cut right through her brain and separated her body from her senses.

It wasn't exactly painful, but then again, she couldn't be sure what she was feeling, except for relief when she lost consciousness.

The numenjax cut off communication a heartbeat or two later, when they realized that reaching out with their mind-circle to welcome her had set off an unexpected reaction.

"Unexpected?" Dr. Tahl had fumed, when Thyal passed on the message from the numenjax, while Confri was still recuperating in medical. "How about dangerous? Damaging? Heavy-handed? Threatening to shred her mind's bond with her body?"

"At least they apologized," M'kar offered. She was seated cross-legged on the other bed in Confri's room, sipping on a mug of something glossy black and smelling of anise.

Dr. Tahl glared at M'kar. Ha'ess, the poison green drac sitting on her shoulder let out a few shrill chirps, ending on a huffing sort of sound. Then the *Defender*'s chief medical offer stomped out of the room. Confri suspected her biological circuity had been cross-linked. She saw sparks trailing from the ends of Dr. Tahl's white hair, and more sparks spun under her cocoa-dark skin. Maybe that was normal for Ankuar?

"I sure hope I'm wrong," M'kar muttered, once the door of Confri's room slid closed.

"About what?" Confri asked. She flinched when her voice rasped.

"M'kar is trying to be funny," Thyal said.

"Le'ankans don't understand humor." M'kar snorted, grinned a little, then scooted to the end of the bed and leaned out, offering her mug. "You might need this. Brea invented this for me when we first met the dracs and I was getting my circuits scrambled with nightly psionic interrogations."

"Thanks, but whatever everybody has been pumping into me finally seems to be working. Just a little thirsty." Confri reached for the tall beaker of sparkling, pale pink, viscous liquid Medtech Brea had given her just after she woke up. She had managed a few sips before M'kar and Thyal came into her room. "What do you hope you're wrong about?"

"M'kar thinks our dracs might be starting to go through puberty. Or at least the females are. I'm of the opinion the stressors are external," Thyal said. In response, Infrenx, his orange, brown, and gold drac crooned softly and snuggled a little closer against his chest.

"Give her the rest of the message before Tahl comes back and throws us out," M'kar said. Barroo chirped, sounding like he agreed with her. That earned grins from everyone.

"As usual, most numenjax communication is with impressions, rather than actual words," he said. "They are sorry to have caused you distress. Your mind fascinates them, and they fear that when they made contact, to drive Granny away, they lingered too long, trying to figure out just what makes you different from the other minds they have been able to touch. They pushed too hard. Or perhaps a better way of expressing it is ..." He shook his head and his eyes narrowed as he visibly searched for the right words.

"They got so excited, they tripped and fell and landed on you, while they were trying to take you into the house to show the adults," M'kar offered.

Thyal rolled his eyes, but a moment later he grinned and nodded. "Close enough."

"So did they figure out anything about me? I know I have a weird Talent. Tell me something I don't know," Confri said, the last sentence more for herself than for them.

"There are portions of your psionic core that are still raw. You suffered a great trauma, and it is a sign of your strength that you did not entirely shut down, that you did not lose access to your Talent, while you heal. They are fascinated by ... the closest word I can come up with is 'multiplicity.' Your multiplicity. But that doesn't make sense."

"Maybe if my mind fractured into a few different people?"

"No. I considered that. Split personalities are more folklore than scientific fact."

"Le'ankans are disgusting that way," M'kar offered. "No mental illness whatsoever among them. That makes it hard for them to understand it in the rest of us."

Again, Thyal rolled his eyes. He was turned enough that he could wink at Confri without M'kar being at the right angle to see.

"They made a promise to you. At least, that is how I take it," he continued after a moment. "They will watch over you while you are here studying the Chute, and will try to keep Granny from pestering you in the future. They also said you will be rewarded for your good stewardship of what Enlo has entrusted to you. They offer the hope of healing, to you and the other injured. And they warned that your reward, your gift, might appear to be a burden."

"Don't ask," M'kar said, when Confri turned to her. "I've been thinking about it, trying to find different interpretations of the images and feelings since they grabbed our heads for a conference call. This is way too close to old prophecies that the Masters are always arguing over, insisting that they aren't complete, they're just bits and pieces of old documents, gathered in one place."

"Unfortunately," Thyal said, "I must agree. Our minds are too limited, and the numenjax joint consciousness is too complex for us to have clear communication all the time."

"On a positive note," Dr. Tahl said, her voice coming through the speaker by the door, making all three and the two dracs jump a little. "Granny will finally leave you alone. If you two are finished, my patient needs some quiet to finish recovering."

"Thank you," Confri said. She supposed the echoing sensation inside her head could be blamed on exhaustion. Every documented encounter with the numenjax was described as being draining and mind-expanding. However, she seriously doubted she was going to get much rest, while she gnawed on the mystery of what the numenjax had promised her.

<div align="center">~~~~~</div>

The day before the *Defender* was to leave Castitarus, Confri had another off-duty day and went to visit the Lores. Jasper and Treinna were finishing up their duty shifts when she arrived, so she wandered the ship, saying farewell to members of the crew who had become friends. She went to the lower cargo bays, to watch M'kar teach self-defense to a group of students younger than Tress. When the class was over, she lingered in the anteroom, waiting for it to be completely quiet. She had a feeling that someone called her name, just outside of hearing range. She hadn't had that feeling since Acon first began withdrawing from their sibling bond. Confri stayed as still as she could, listening. The hunger to regain that feeling of being in contact with another mind made her pause and listen, near the cargo bays.

A ruckus erupted in the other cargo bay. Confri staggered back two steps, momentarily confused by the sensation of being inside a dark, small place -- and something huge banged against the walls surrounding her. Shouts and flickers of colors and a sudden cacophony of squeals and chattering shattered that sensation and drew her attention to the cargo bay where some crew had been at work. She was nearly bowled over when the cargo bay door slid open and three crew hurtled through, swatting at a cloud of dracs who spun around them.

That calling sensation drew her into the bay, where Granny and five other dracs were assaulting a cargo bin that sat crooked on a ramp into a shuttle. Dr. Darias had mentioned expecting a load of samples taken from different levels of the tunnels leading down into the numenjax lair. The geology team from the *Defender* was preparing to send it to the *Perelandra*.

Why would the dracs be interested in a bin full of rocks?

Granny and her minions dive-bombed the cargo bin. They could teleport, so Confri imagined there wasn't enough open space inside the bin for them to teleport inside and snatch whatever they wanted. Were they trying to knock it open? Or knock it over? Maybe they didn't want the rocks to leave the *Defender*? Maybe Granny was just crazy enough, after having been defeated by the numenjax, she didn't want anything from Castitarus on the ship?

"The sooner Jasper gets that drac-proof fence up and working," a crewman said, stepping into the doorway behind Confri, "the better for everybody's sanity." He snorted when she turned to look at him. "If we're lucky, the little lunatics will knock themselves out and we'll have some peace for a few hours."

Confri grinned in agreement and turned back to watch. She had to give Granny and her minions points for determination and persistence. Just as she finished turning around, they succeeded, knocking over the bin, off the ramp, so it tumbled onto its side. Granny caroled in triumph. The largest of the dracs, a deep blue with black streaks on its wings, dropped down to perch on the side of the bin and pried at the latch.

In seconds, the lid opened and fell back, so all sorts of rock samples spilled across the deck. Granny dove and snatched up a rough, oval rock more than half her size. She managed to rise up for three beats of her wings, then let out a piteous and yet furious squawk and let go of the rock. It hit the pile of other rocks and tumbled down. A plum-colored drac dove down and tried to clutch the rock, but it only got up off the deck maybe half a meter before it cried out in pain, let go of the rock, and fluttered away at a crooked angle.

Confri and the crewman watched this performance as each drac tried to fly away with that specific rock. They ignored all the others. Granny tried a second time, crying out in pain as she let go of the rock. She spiraled upward with more energy than Confri thought possible, after the outcry she had made.

"Something weird about that rock," she muttered. Without thinking, she darted forward and reached for the rock, which by now had tumbled a few meters away from pile. The crewman cried out warning. Confri sensed the incoming body before she heard the rasping cry. She dove for the rock, clutched it to her chest, and rolled.

Music strummed through her body. Through a shimmering spectrum haze, she saw Granny come back for a second try. The silver drac dove, talons outstretched -- and bounced off the haze of colors. Hissing, she fluttered upward again, then popped out.

"Forget the fence. M'kar needs to follow through on her threat to make that one a belt," the crewman exclaimed, as he hurried forward to help Confri up.

She didn't want to let go of the rock. The song had faded from her ears, but it hummed in her blood. The colors had left her sight, but she thought she could taste them in the air.

Maybe she had hit her head when she dove for the rock?

More crew came in, grumbling or laughing about the mess the dracs had made. She tucked the rock inside her uniform jacket as she helped the crew put everything back into the cargo bin, then slide it up the ramp into the shuttle. Just as she thought, they were sending this selection of rock samples to the *Perelandra*. Confri knew this was the point in every story she had ever read where the foolish, perhaps rebellious heroines got themselves in trouble by doing something secretive, but suddenly she understood why those idiots broke rules. The rock *sang* to her. Energy hummed from it. She was probably the only one who could hear or feel or taste the energy, almost fizzing in her blood. Dr. Darias would wear the rock into dust with all the tests she would run on it, and something inside Confri howled not to allow that to happen. She promised herself she would write up a report for Darias, but she wasn't going to let the rock out of her sight. Not until she had thoroughly examined it in her own way.

She thought about telling Jasper what she had found. He and Cullin were probably the only people on both ships who would understand why the rock fascinated her. She decided not to worry him. He had enough on his plate, with that desperately needed drac-proof fence, and the psionic Talent waiting to blossom in Tress. The rock sang quietly to *her*, no one else.

She wrapped up the rock and put it in a smaller travel box, marked it for her special attention, and put it on the shuttle to go to the *Perelandra*. It would be safe in the sciences lab until she figured out what to do with it. After she told Captain Minerbec about it. Keeping dangerous secrets was something foolish heroines always did, until the monster hidden in the box or the egg or behind the long-forgotten door emerged to rain carnage down on everyone. She trusted her captain to in turn trust that she knew what she was doing.

At least, Confri hoped she knew what she was doing.

She enjoyed her off-duty day with Japer and Treinna and Tress, and only occasionally thought about the rock and the song that had spilled through her blood, and the odd haze of colors that somehow kept Granny from hitting her.

~~~~~

By the third time she woke up that night, positive she heard a baby crying, Confri had had enough.

"What did I eat that I shouldn't have?" she mumbled.

Just like the previous two times, as soon as she was awake the sound of crying stopped. Usually that proved it had just been a bad dream. But she could usually hold onto her dreams long enough after waking to *know* she had been dreaming. Muffling a groan, she rolled over and out of her bed. On the other side of the bedroom of their cabin, her roommate, Astra, let out a rattling little snore.

When the snore ended ... she swore she heard a sound that shouldn't be there. Did the crying continue? It didn't exactly sound like a baby crying, now that she was awake. Maybe she wasn't awake, she was only dreaming she was awake?

Maybe she just needed to find something to settle her stomach. Or she needed to go somewhere more private, and quiet, to implement some Le'ankan disciplines, and find out what was really triggering her strange dreams. Maybe she had picked up something that lodged in her subconscious and only niggled at her when she was asleep?

Sighing, she tugged on civvies over her sleeping shorts and shirt, and slippers on her bare feet, and left the cabin. Her roommate needed her sleep. Astra was on the team helping to untangle Castitaran society and came back to the ship from her on-planet shifts exhausted. If she wasn't scanning and translating historical documents, she was dealing with a dozen calls for help at a time, from the Castitaran healers and clan and guild leaders as they tried to learn to use the new technology provided to them by Fleet. Confri was grateful she was an engineer and not a sociologist.
~~~~~

The corridor was much quieter than her cabin. Confri stopped and held her breath and extended her senses.

There. That was the sound. Definitely not a baby crying. Yet she couldn't term it any kind of energy she had ever encountered, either. Certainly, she had experienced some strange cross-circuiting of her senses, when she analyzed heretofore unknown energies. Was the time-lock Chute acting up?

Confri shuddered at the multiple possibilities that thought spun through her mind, and padded down the corridors to the mess hall. Where was that sound coming from?

She tapped the beverage dispenser control, then paused, trying to decide which hot drink she wanted. Something to soothe and put her to sleep, and silence the crying, thereby proving it was merely a bad food reaction? Or something to make her more alert? Meaning she might still be padding around the quiet ship when the night shift turned to day shift. Honestly, what were her chances of getting back to sleep with that sound bothering her every time she drifted off?

Something to wake her up, definitely. Confri scorched her tongue on the first sip of thitpan tea. She grinned, despite the spicy-sour taste that scoured away that thick, sleeping-with-the-mouth-open sensation.

And the baby kept crying.

But not a real … no, that wasn't the right word. It wasn't a Human baby, but that didn't mean the sound wasn't a baby. There was something … Confri shook her head and slipped a cover on the cup of tea and headed back out into the corridor. There was something *other* about the sound. Now that she was fully, stingingly awake, images accompanied the sound. This was more than just sensory data manifesting as physical senses. A chill settled into her fingers and toes, despite the warmth of the corridor. She felt like she was in a cold, dark space, surrounded by hard surfaces.

The darkness echoed. She stumbled when she heard a click, just like the box had clicked when she put the rock into it, to send to the ship.

"Please, Enlo, I'm not hallucinating, am I?" she whispered. Just to be sure she wasn't still dreaming, she took a big mouthful of the tea. She nearly choked on the bitterness that scoured her sinuses. "Was it singing to me?"

She flinched at the sound of her voice. She hadn't meant to say that aloud. It was one thing to get sensations of energy and liken them to sensory impressions, but it was something else altogether to confuse those crossed signals for the real thing.

But what if?

Confri shuddered as she stepped into the lift and tapped the controls to take her up two decks to the lab where the rock waited for her. She remembered how the dracs had fought to take that one rock away. Why? What was special about it? Other than the energy that sang through her blood … and made her feel as if she had made someone happy when she touched it?

"When did I get that impression?" she murmured.

No one answered. She hadn't spoken loudly enough to alert the ship's system. Silence accompanied her as she got out of the lift and walked down the corridor to the lab. The baby, if it was a baby, had stopped crying. Did it know she was coming to get it out of the box?

"Great. Living rocks along with dragons," she murmured as she stepped into the lab. She walked into the interior storage area, tapped in her security code and held still for the retina scan. The locker keyed to her pattern clicked open. She blinked, positive the storage box glowed softly for a few seconds, before the light automatically came up in the storage room.

A sigh whispered through her mind. Confri shuddered with the sense of relief in that sound. Yet it wasn't a *sound*. It was entirely psionic. She flipped up the lid of the box, reached in, and cupped the rock in both hands.

It felt … smoother than when she put it in the box.

It vibrated.

Hello? Is there anyone in there?

A chirping kind of giggle washed over her, eliciting a purring kind of chuckle from deep inside. Confri didn't know she could even make a sound like that. Someone, or something had heard her, and it was very happy.

No. Wait. There was something wrong with her if there was something inside a rock and she let it make her that happy, without any explanation.

Maybe when her bond with Acon snapped, it had caused her some mental and emotional damage that was only making itself felt now, two years later?

The sensation of incredible cold pulsed through her again. Whatever was inside the rock didn't like being cold. Was there such a thing as a sentient rock?

The warmest spot in the lab, besides her, was the steaming mug of thitpan tea. Confri walked over to where she had put down her mug, pried up the lid, and held the rock in the thin, swirling column of steam.

No, that was stupid. It wasn't enough. Unless she poured the hot liquid over the rock.

A little more thought. She put the rock down in a bin, then opened a cabinet and brought out a thermal sheet with a heating/cooling element in it. She set the temperature for ten degrees higher than body temperature and wrapped the sheet around the rock. She put it back in the bin, rested her elbows on the counter, and waited.

Her back ached a little, and she shivered in the chill air of the powered-down lab. Confri considered taking the rock back to her cabin. No. Besides violating security protocols and common sense, she didn't need to inflict whatever might happen on Astra. Her roommate needed her sleep. Who wanted to be awakened by … whatever was about to happen?

A hissing sound brought her upright. With her forefinger, she poked aside the thermal wrap.

Her mouth dropped open.

The rock had turned to sand and was sheeting off … something in softly glimmering jewel tones of blue and gold and green. That explained the hissing sound.

At least, she hoped so.

The lab lights were too dim. They wouldn't come up until she ordered them, and she wasn't ready to do that, and alert security sensors. No one was supposed to be in here. Confri moved closer, even knowing this was the point in horror stories when the mysterious object split open and something horrific leaped out to bite off her head. Gingerly, she tugged down on the thermal sheet a little more. And gasped.

It was an egg.

What was an egg doing inside a rock?

Had the dracs been trying to rescue the egg? Maybe an egg had fallen into thickening mud and got coated?

Why did the dracs have a hard time picking it up?

She wished she had spent more of her time with Treinna, M'kar and Thyal, asking about the care of dracs before they hatched. All she knew was that drac eggs needed to be fed, by sitting in piles of food. Hopefully just plant matter.

"Okay, little guy, I don't know what kind of trouble you're in, but … looks like you're stuck with me. Are you feeling better?"

Taking a deep breath to brace herself, she slipped her hands under the egg and lifted it out of the thermal sheet. It glowed softly, shimmering through the spectrum. Confri watched the shifting of colors, fascinated, until an odd twisting sensation in her stomach startled her. Common sense told her if she could feel when the egg was cold … maybe now she felt its hunger?

"Time to go to school, I suppose," she whispered to whoever was inside. She made a pouch of her shirt to hold the egg and keep it warm, while trying to remember everything Treinna had told her about feeding eggs before they hatched.

Every time ships met up in the course of missions, there was always an exchange of data. If Enlo was merciful, M'kar had made available for general education a basic primer on the care and feeding of dracs. It made sense, considering how important dracs would be in both driving away the Hivers, and hopefully awaking the prisoners of their cocoons. Confri spoke awake the lab's computer. In less than ten minutes, she had the information she needed. She found it fascinating.

Drac eggs were fed during the gestation, just like Treinna had said. The duration of the time from laying to hatching was unknown, because the first eggs had just been laid at Anwesta Medical Station. Eggs had been fed through the generations on Draxonis by burying them in plant matter, which was then absorbed through the shells. Wait, she had touched that leathery, soft, jewel-toned shell with her bare hands. That made her squirm a little. Had the hungry baby drac inside … fed off her, just a little?

A few more questions and Confri had the nutrient requirements. She sent them to the synthesis lab, then carried the egg down the corridor. In a few minutes, the synthesis slot produced a slow stream of what looked like slightly wilted, pale green and purple-streaked berries. Confri half-filled a box with them, put the egg inside, then stopped the flow and stored the formula for future use. Then … she wasn't quite sure what to do. She didn't want to let the egg out of her sight, but she squirmed a little at the thought of bringing it into the cabin with her and Astra. Her roommate really was a lovely, understanding, fun person, but Confri just didn't know if she would accept the egg's presence in stride, or be slightly freaked out by it.

Especially when Confri told her how and where she had found it.

A soft sigh of satisfaction whispered through her mind. Was it her imagination, or did the egg sink down a little in the food pellets? Was the little drac inside that hungry? The glow had faded. She wondered if that was a side effect of filling a need, or maybe she had poisoned the egg and didn't realize it yet?

Tentatively, she touched the egg, just three fingers. The glow softly, slowly returned, and traveled up her fingers, across the back of her hand.

Maybe she was just tired, or this whole encounter was doing strange things to her brain, but she had the hazy impression that the egg ... liked her. Wanted to be with her.

That settled it. She clutched the box to her chest and trotted down the corridor, back to the life sciences lab, where she settled down at the terminal to read everything she could about dracs, drac eggs, and hatching. First, though, she revised her report for Captain Minerbec. Always better to keep the captain updated on every strange event. The less she had to apologize for if something ... bizarre happened, the better.

~~~~~

When Astra came looking for her two hours later, Confri had fallen asleep at the terminal, the last page she had read still displayed. She leaned over the box, with her hand inside, touching the egg. A softly pulsing, rainbow shimmer stroked up and down her arm. She found that comforting when she woke up.

Captain Minerbec wanted to see her. The summons had come to their cabin and woke Astra. Had the captain read Confri's report before breakfast? The thought of breakfast made her stomach pinch and growl loudly enough to make Astra laugh. She looked at the egg, looked at the page of the report on the screen, and advised Confri to wash up, change her clothes, and get something in her stomach before facing the captain.

~~~~~

"Your record says your psionic potential hasn't been fully explored. This might be part of it," Captain Minerbec offered, once he and Confri had gone over everything that had happened to her, all her impressions and theories that hadn't gone into her basic report. "I don't fault you for any of the steps you took, after the animosity that drac displayed toward you. I just wish you had discovered the egg before the *Defender* went through the Chute."

"The next logical step is to head for Anwesta." Confri nodded. "Between the need to understand dracs in all phases of the life cycle, and the need for more dracs to focus on cocoons and help awaken the victims of the Hivers... honestly, sir, I'm going to need guidance from those with more experience if I'm not going to totally knot up the whole thing."

"One question, or maybe it's a problem." Her captain tapped the controls in the surface of his desk, and the report lifted off as a hologram, highlighting a section that came directly from the initial dossier of what the *Defender* and *Corona* had discovered about dracs. "There should be three eggs. So where are the other two? Still hidden in rocks inside that cargo bin of samples? Which leads to the next question. Who's going to be forcibly adopted before we find them?"

"What happens if we don't find them? And why didn't the *Defender* realize some of their dracs had mated and laid eggs?" Confri sighed. "If Granny was trying to keep the egg from leaving the ship, why didn't she communicate that need to M'kar? It's crazy, but my impression is she didn't want the egg around, at all, not that she was protecting it."

Captain Minerbec frowned more deeply. "I had a long talk with Captain Arroyan, after you were singled out by that little silver menace. She told me all I could ever want to know about dracs and getting ambushed by hatching eggs. Do we assume the other two eggs remain on Castitarus? And how soon will they hatch?"

"According to Lt. M'kar's report, the shell should look like gems, or crystalized sugar, ready to shatter into dust shortly before hatching. This egg is still soft, pliable in most places. The little guy inside is dang hungry, too."

"Ah ... are you sure it's male, or is that just a figure of speech?"

She paused to think a moment. "Just an impression."

"Not a good place to be," her captain mused. He rubbed his face with the heels of his hands and sighed. "Well ... there's a courier ship leaving in four days. If we can't find the other two eggs by that time, to send with you, we don't dare delay you any longer."

~~~~~

By the third day, with no success in the search for the other two eggs, Confri wondered if the egg had done something to her brain. She was making enormous strides in studying and assessing the energy fluctuations in the Chute. Could she credit her theoretical bond with the egg for her increased sensitivity to energy fluctuations
~~~~~

and refined ability to hear the "song" of the equipment and the frequencies traveling through space? She didn't worry that no other eggs had been found, because something, maybe the egg, told her there were no other eggs. She couldn't say it *told* her in so many words, yet there was communication growing between them.

She played with the idea, late at night when she was drowsing into sleep, that maybe this wasn't a drac egg at all, but maybe Granny had been trying to stop a numenjax egg from leaving Castitarus. As she hovered on the verge of sleep, that wordless impression urged her to trust the numenjax. There was no way they could lose an egg, or have one misplaced and sent away by accident, so if they wanted to send away an egg, trusting Humans to raise a numenjax child, there had to be a reason. She didn't need to worry. She was doing just what she was supposed to do, and there was nothing Granny could have done to interfere.

When sleep came each night, she dreamed of laughing with someone who felt like a best friend she had known all her life. On the third and fourth nights after discovering the egg, she heard Acon's voice in her dreams. What he said, she didn't know, but she felt his sorrow.

She thought several times about requesting an audience with the numenjax, to test her theories, maybe get some advice. Each time, she decided not to. With that looming deadline speeding closer, she needed to get as much work done as she could studying the Chute before she left. Besides, M'kar and Thyal were gone, and the few Talents who had been chosen to train to act as intermediaries between Humans and numenjax weren't strong enough to shield her. She didn't need to get her circuits scrambled again, thanks very much.

On the morning after the deadline passed, she packed her gear, synthesized enough food pellets to hold the egg for the journey, and did twice as much work on the Chute. Her friends in the Gate team and Engineering teased her that she had given them enough to work with for the next planetary year, and she could go on as long a vacation as she wanted. Lunch was a low-key sort of farewell party, with hugs and some teary eyes and jokes. She would miss her crewmates and friends, even as she quivered inside with the feeling that the universe was opening up around her. Anything was possible.

The courier ship had room for six crew, with the hold half-filled with scientific samples, documents, and disks full of data. The other half of the hold was reserved on every trip for whatever the survey teams on Draxonis, on the other end of the Chute, would have ready to send through the second Chute to the Alliance. Confri settled into the bunkroom and prepared for the transition down the Chute to Draxonis.

She wondered if the egg would change how she perceived Chute travel. The adopted drac parents on the *Defender* didn't feel the transition anymore. If the brain suckage that occurred in the bond between drac and Human rewired their brains, whatever was happening between her and the egg would affect her as well.

The egg in its padded box was strapped into the corner of her bunk against the wall, by her head, where any jolting or dropping or twisting of the courier ship wouldn't knock it loose. Most of the time, the wild ride down a Chute was mostly perceived and not truly physical in the bumps and jolts, rises and falls and spins. Depending on how badly the pilot's perceptions were compromised, a slightly bumpy ride could turn into a bone-rattling ten minutes that could feel like an hour.

The pilot called from the cockpit to announce the ship was entering the Chute. Confri lay down on her bunk and closed her eyes. She exhaled a sigh as rainbows swirled behind her eyelids. Soft pastels, with sparkles along the edges. She opened her eyes and flinched as the rainbows wrapped around her, as if trying to fasten her to the bunk. Two heartbeats, and the colors faded. It wasn't over with already, was it?

So, had the egg influenced her in some way? She made mental notes during the remainder of the journey down the Chute. Everything she experienced had to be reported, because her experiences were adding to the slowly growing data dealing with dracs.

"The sooner you come out of there and can talk with me, the better," she murmured. Then she laughed. What made her think her drac would be able to talk to her in words she could understand? Nowhere in the drac manual did she find any hope that the occupant of her egg would be able to communicate any more clearly than the *Defender*'s dracs.

"All clear," the pilot announced.

Confri got up from her bunk and headed for the ship's lounge. This was where she and the crew would spend most of their time on the trip from the other end of the Draxonis Chute to Anwesta and Le'anka. The lounge was common room, mess hall, entertainment area, and gym. Other than the cargo compartment, the only other compartments in the crew area of the courier ship were the washroom and the medical bay, with room for one patient to lie down and be monitored by the automated medical equipment. If anyone else was injured or sick, they would have to make do on the recliners in the lounge or retreat to the bunk room.

Four steps took her out of the bunk room and into the lounge. She smiled, knowing she could get back to the egg in just a few seconds. No more moments of panic like she had experienced on the *Perelandra*, after half an hour of absence from the egg. She only needed two instances of that aching feeling of loneliness before she fashioned a padded bag on a long strap, to keep the egg with her while on duty.

During the voyage, she would help with general housekeeping and cooking chores, when she wasn't studying the egg and the drac manual, and making notes to add to the general knowledge. Couriers were small, built for speed and stealth. She was the only passenger, so she would be pretty much on her own when the crew of two were either on duty or sleeping.

Shad Green was the pilot and his twin sister, Shara was co-pilot and medic. Shara came back to greet Confri and held out the medical scanner as she was settling into one of the lounge chairs.

"Any difference in Chute transition?" she asked, as the wand hummed and colors flashed up and down the length of it.

"Some. Not what I expected, though." Confri braced for a slew of questions, but Shara just nodded and watched the readings on the flat side of the wand. "No nausea. This time I got a light show for just a few seconds. The *Defender*'s crew bonded with dracs reported that all reactions to the interdimensional warping of the Chute were negated."

"Maybe that's the difference between a drac in the egg and one that's hatched." She pursed her lips, studying the readings, then shrugged. "My psi isn't strong enough for duty on Anwesta, but I have some friends from the Academy who did have enough to be assigned. Every day is something new to add to the growing data. I'll try not to make a pest of myself, but you have to admit you're a tempting subject."

"No, the egg that latched onto me is the temptation."

They laughed together. Confri didn't mind that Shara hoped for a chance to study the egg. Maybe get ahead of her friends on the front lines of studying the dracs. She brought out the box protecting the egg and they discussed some of her theories. They were still studying some of the readings on the medical scanner when Shad announced they were settling into orbit around Draxonis. The survey ships orbiting the planet had signaled the courier when it first emerged from the Chute. Their newest batch of reports weren't ready yet. There would be a delay of at least four hours until the courier could dock with the largest ship, pick up the samples, download the reports, and head through the second Chute.

The delay didn't matter, because the courier ship had to wait until the teams on the planet gathered up enough native plants to fill the second cargo bay on the courier. The food was destined for the dracs on Anwesta. Confri wondered if, by the time they reached the medical station, Granny would still be in a foul mood after her humiliating defeat at the hands (paws? claws?) of the numenjax. What were the chances she had been so infuriated by her defeat, she had skipped ship when the *Defender* stopped at Draxonis on its way back to Alliance territory? What were the chances Granny would sense the presence of Confri and the egg, even at orbital distance, would teleport up here, and start her harassment all over again?

"Better not to ask, and keep a low profile," Shara said, when Confri voiced her thoughts. "Don't even think about her. Dracs haven't been hanging around with Humans long enough for us to know everything they can do. Or can't do."

When the cargo of harvested roots and stalks and leaves was transferred from the central survey ship, the *Velocity*, a passenger popped out of the largest bin. A mottled brown and green drac hopped up on the lid of the bin, then leaped up to one of the anchoring loops hanging from the ceiling and sat there, regarding Confri and Shad.

"You are not coming back with us." He gave Confri a sideways look. "Is he?"

"Just how are we going to stop him?" She flinched as the drac leaped off the loop, spread his wings and glided over to within arm's length of her face -- then popped out.

"Does that give you the jitters like it does me? Living things should not be able to do that. Even if they do look like miniature dragons."

"Or is it more that we think it's wrong because Humans can't?"

"Hmm ..." He grinned. "You're probably right."

A yelp from the living area of the courier ship indicated where the drac had teleported. Confri fought a sudden sense of panic and ran, through the two open hatches, nearly tripping over the high thresholds, until she got to the bunkroom.

The drac perched on the edge of her bunk, peering into the box. He turned slowly and regarded her, eyes sparkling with swirls of green and blue. Supposedly those were peaceful colors. He wasn't afraid or angry, but she supposed a drac could be peaceful while planning mischief, if those plans amused him.

"You are not taking that baby ... are you?" She wondered if her transfer was about to stop right here, with a drac confiscating the egg. Just how could she get it back, with a whole planet to search?

The drac raised up on his hind legs and looked into the box again.

The egg glowed, the flare of light and energy strong, and quick. No chance of it being an optical illusion this time.

The drac let out a squawk and stumbled backwards, fumbled for one second as he tipped and fell off the bunk, then popped out.

It didn't come back, though Confri stood there, holding her breath and waiting until sparkles appeared around the edges of her vision.

"What do you think that was about?" Shara asked.

Confri squeaked, releasing the held breath. She shrugged. "I'm not in link or bond or whatever with dracs, so don't ask me." She wanted to reach into the box and cradle the egg, but she was afraid to move her arms and show just how much she was trembling.

Was it just her imagination, or had that drac been *frightened* by the egg?

~~~~~

That night, Confri dreamed she kept trying to talk to the egg, but a voice composed of stone and water and fire kept whispering, "Ssshhh."

Just that. No other sounds, no other message. Just to be quiet.

So she wrote notes on her dreams in her growing report, and prepared herself for a long talk with the drac experts on Anwesta.

~~~~~

"Message for you," Shad called back to Confri, two days after they had come through the Draxonis Chute. "Transferring."

"Thanks." Confri put down the bowl she had just emptied into the baking pan and put it into the makeshift oven.

There were quite a few things about the living arrangements of the courier ship that were not quite regulation. She suspected the inspectors gave the courier teams some leeway. Anything to make their solitary near-light-speed journeys easier to bear. Such as indulging Shad and Shara's love of baking. She had been happy to add to their cookbook with a few recipes she had created. Shad joked that when they were ready to retire from the courier service, they could publish the book and become famous throughout the universe for the recipes bringing the flavors of several dozen worlds to the entire Alliance.

Now that the quick bread was safely in the oven, she could focus on the message that Shad had sent to her tablet. When the courier ship emerged from the Chute, she had sent a message to Lt. M'kar, telling her about the cargo bin, Granny's attack on it, the rock that called to her, and the egg that emerged from it. She had personal details and questions that couldn't be included in that official, scientific, facts-only report she had sent to the drac team on Anwesta.

With only one more day of travel until reaching Anwesta, Confri had to wonder why it had taken so long for the relays to get her communication to the *Defender*, and for M'kar to respond.

Lt. M'kar started with an apology. The *Defender* had been sent on shore leave on Mendax, a world that was still waiting for official Alliance membership entry. Someone, somewhere in the bureaucracy felt something was not *wrong*, but not quite right, either. The *Defender* had a mission of thoroughly investigating the colony to ensure it was a safe shore leave location. M'kar was joking, hopefully, when she said her ship and crew's reputation ensured that if anything bizarre was hidden on Mendax, they would uncover it. She sent a separate document, responding to Confri's questions and observations about the egg, and had copied Dr. Garion Dulit, head drac liaison on Anwesta, so he would know what Confri was bringing. She urged Confri to trust Dulit completely, as he was a classmate of hers from the Academy.

I'm very concerned about your impression Granny was trying to take the egg, possibly to harm it, M'kar wrote. *I've interrogated our teacher dracs until my head hurts and they're too skittish to stay in the same room with me. It's difficult interpreting the images and impressions I get from them. Part of that could be the scare that the numenjax put into them. Granny is furious with them, and that's anathema in drac culture. They don't want me angry, either, if they don't tell me what I want to know. But they can't tell me. I can't decide if they honestly can't remember the incident, or if they've been ordered a thousand ways from yesterday, and very sternly, not to tell us two-legs-no-wings what happened and why.*

The existence of one egg worries me. If there is a mated pair among our twelve teacher dracs, how did we not notice? The mated pairs we observed on Draxonis are very obvious. How did the female lay her eggs without a drac celebration on the ship? There are just so many holes in this slowly growing picture of drac knowledge. We're going to need to rewrite the whole book, obviously. I'm afraid Granny blew so many circuits when her plot to rule the numenjax disintegrated, she's entirely irrational, and it's affecting all the dracs under her. This isn't good news for the cocoon project on Anwesta. Dulit has been warned to keep a close eye on Granny, and Jasper is hard at work on the drac-proof fence, in case we need to confine her. Hopefully a field that keeps a drac from teleporting will also cut off communication with other dracs. It won't do us much good to keep her locked up if she can still cause mischief by remote control.

I'm sorry. That isn't much help. One theory is that three eggs were laid on Castitarus during our mission, but the same incident that coated your egg destroyed the other two eggs. That could be enough to traumatize adult dracs. When we proposed the theory, our young dracs gave us big-eyed, horrified looks, and they needed a lot of cuddling and comforting.

Hopefully we'll be back from shore leave durance vile before your egg hatches. Until then, you can depend on Dulit. He is setting up equipment to study and monitor your egg as it matures. Sorry, but you're going to be the focus of great speculations. Granny could throw another hissy and try to confiscate the egg the moment you step foot on Anwesta. Don't let the old biddy dominate you. Keep the numenjax in the front of your thoughts, and that should drive her away.

Enlo guide and guard you.

"Well, that's not much help, but they tried," she murmured to the egg. Confri wasn't in the mood now to read the attachment with all the official, scientific responses to her questions and observations.

The possibility that there was something emotionally and mentally wrong with the matriarch of the dracs, on whom rested the possibility to someday awaken the victims trapped inside cocoons ... was depressing. It worried and frightened her.

That night, in her dreams, the egg's occupant whispered encouragement without words. Acon hovered in the shadows, just on the edge of her vision, and smiled at her. Just waiting. She couldn't wait to see him, even if all she could do was sit with him as he stood vigil over his sweetheart and their crewmates' cocoons.

Behind all that comfort, she had the soft, tantalizing impression of someone ... laughing. Like a delightful, slightly mischievous child would laugh, holding onto a secret.

~~~~~

The courier ship reached Anwesta just before lunchtime, courier ship time, the next day. A white drac with lavender shading and a dark blue drac popped into the waiting area while Confri was going through the medical checks and scans and identification checks. They swirled around her several times, nearly scraping the ceiling of the room. She found it interesting that the woman running the check-in process ignored the dracs. Until they were gone. Then she met Confri's gaze and rolled her eyes, shook her head once, and continued with her task.

"Does that happen often?" Confri had to ask.

"Poki and Cobalt are in and out everywhere on the station. They're very well-behaved. There's a big difference between their poking into everything, and what the bigger, older dracs do. If they ever leave their habitat or the cocoon rooms."

A white-haired man waited in the next room, when Confri cleared all the checks. The white-and-lavender drac now perched on his shoulder. She guessed this was Dr. Garion Dulit before he even introduced himself. He gave one long look to the closed box holding the egg, then gestured to the door into the station's corridor. As they walked, he gave her a running introduction to the station, the safety procedures and regulations, the layout, the fastest way to the socializing areas, the residential blocks, the off-limits areas. Confri knew most of this from the introductory packet. She appreciated being able to match diagrams with physical reality.

"This is basically our lair, drac parents' home base," he announced.

They stepped into a long room. The far wall was a transparent
~~~~~

panel looking down on the main cocoon "greenhouse." The aroma of rich soil, green growing things, and humidity wrapped around Confri, soothing. The air was constantly cleansed and filtered and balanced. She took several deep, slow breaths as Dulit led her over to a cluster of lounging chairs. A small food services cubicle sat in one corner. Rows of deep growth bins lined several walls, full of plants she recognized as imported from Draxonis, to grow foodstuffs to support drac health.

Their quarters were in a portion of Anwesta designated for expansion, as the services of the station increased. As more Humans were adopted by hatching dracs, the numbers of drac parents on duty in the effort to reach Humans trapped in cocoons would also increase, and the need to house them. For now, the long room with its drac play area of loops hanging from the ceiling and perches and haphazard towers of boxes for nesting, the medical equipment and other facilities, was more than enough for the three assigned here. Confri made four now.

Dulit asked her to open the box, so he could examine the egg. His eyes narrowed as he looked into it. "When did you last top off the food pellets?"

"Last night before I turned in." She shrugged and looked down into the box. She supposed the level just below midpoint in the egg might be discouraging to him, but she was amazed the level of remaining pellets wasn't lower. "His appetite has actually slowed down."

"Uh huh." His smile widened and warmed a little. "I'm not criticizing. You're probably wondering ..." He tipped his head to study the drac sitting on his shoulder. Poki stayed hunkered down, her tail wrapped around his neck, her forepaws gripping the shoulder of his jacket, and stared at the egg. Dulit sighed. "I'm sorry, but we're in entirely new territory here."

"Meaning?" Confri watched the little drac, whose eyes were a dark shade of blue, touched with slowly swirling streaks of yellow. Once her drac had hatched and she could touch its mind, she would be able to interpret the emotions in the colors of drac eyes. Right now, she wasn't sure she wanted to know what Poki was thinking, or feeling, as she stared at the egg.

He sighed again. "I think ... that's not a drac egg."

She shuddered at this confirmation of her growing suspicions. "So I was right? Granny was trying to get the egg off the *Defender*?"

She took a deep breath. "This is a numenjax egg? But why would they send an egg to us? Why so secretively?"

"Considering how Granny feels about the numenjax? It was probably the only way they could do it, without her interfering more than she did, and causing damage. As for *why* the numenjax did it … who knows?" He reached up to scratch down Poki's back. The little drac hunkered down lower. Her eyes half-closed, his touch visibly soothing.

"Garion." A man's voice came from the speaker strip in the ceiling. "Sorry, couldn't distract --"

A silver blur popped into the room. It circled Confri and Dulit twice. Poki let out squeaks of very evident fear. Granny darted down, aiming for the box.

Confri scooped up the egg and cradled it against her chest. The glow of contact burst out, enveloping her so she almost lost her breath from surprise. This was a repeat of the colors that day she found the rock. Cubed.

Granny collided with the expanding light and bounced backward in mid-air. She let out a shriek of utter astonishment. Her eyes went nearly white, with green speckles. She retreated behind Dulit's head and hung in mid-air, shrieking and scolding and spitting.

"Enough!" Dulit shouted. He leaped to his feet and spread his arms as he turned to face Granny. Poki leaped off his shoulder and popped out, vanishing. "Out." He pointed at the wall. Confri supposed when it came to creatures who could teleport, doors didn't matter. "Get out. You're not welcome here until you can be polite. You hear me? Out!"

Granny's voice rose another octave and her eyes closed with the force of her shrieks, until suddenly she ran out of breath. She drooped, then with a very clear sob, she turned a somersault in mid-air, flipped her tail at them in dismissal, and popped out of sight.

"What was that about?" Confri whispered, and cradled the egg a little closer.

"I could say the same." Dulit gestured at her, from head to toe.

She looked down at herself and held her breath as the glow slowly faded, as if being absorbed into her skin. She suddenly felt very wobbly, and was glad she was sitting down.

Shouldn't she be worried she was either delusional, suffering a brain lesion, or something was taking over her mind?

"How soon does the brain suckage start in?" she whispered, and let the egg slide down to sit in her lap, with both hands resting over it.

"Not until baby hatches."

"What's happening to me?"

"That is not a drac egg."

"That's not an explanation!" She flinched when her voice seemed to bounce off the ceiling.

"Granny very clearly wants that thing off the station."

The door to the common room slid open. A tall, caramel-skinned man walked in, with Cobalt perched on his shoulder. This had to be Flinders, the second of the three drac parents on Anwesta. The third was Aeola, a psi-trained medi-counselor.

"Got some backwash from Granny's tantrum," Flinders said, with a shrug and an apologetic smile. "Welcome to Anwesta." He nodded at the egg in her lap. "Were the troublemakers right?"

"If Granny's snit was any confirmation," Dulit said with a sigh. "Definitely." Poki popped back in and landed with an audible smack on his shoulder. He grinned and stroked the little drac, who wrapped her tail around his neck and cuddled close.

Flinders whistled. "All right, so what do we do?"

"Send her back to Castitarus?"

"What? Why?" Confri burst out.

"Yeah, why?" Flinders dropped down to one knee next to her chair. Cobalt purred softly and reached out with his long neck to nuzzle Confri's shoulder. "Do you really think the big ones would have allowed an egg to be *stolen* by Granny? They sent it away, snuck it into the cargo bin. They had to know where an egg would automatically be sent. Especially if everyone would assume from the start that it was a drac egg."

Confri swallowed hard, grateful Flinders was making it easier on her to accept what had only been a supposition. "If they wanted the egg here," she said, trying not to whisper, trying not to shriek, "then why didn't they just tell M'kar? They were talking to her."

When Aeola joined them a short time later, she came up with a theory that seemed to make sense, even though Confri still found it a little hard to accept. Working from the premise that the numenjax couldn't be bossed around by Granny, and she couldn't get away with anything where they were concerned, then logic said this was part of the numenjax plan. If they could get the egg into the cargo bin, logic said they could get it into the bin going to their chosen destination. Meaning they didn't want those samples and the egg on the *Defender*. So they wanted someone on the *Perelandra*, not the *Defender*, to bond with the numenjax when it hatched. Confri had thought she heard someone calling her that day before she took the egg. If she really had heard the baby crying, and bonding seemed to be happening before birth, logic said the numenjax wanted her, specifically.

They didn't have much more time for theorizing, between getting Confri settled in her quarters and taking her on a tour of the station on their way to have dinner with Commodore Roop, the commander of Anwesta.

Granny popped in four times on their way to the dining room at the very top of the station. Each time she hovered in the corridor a good four or five meters ahead of their group, glaring balefully at them, somehow managing to fly backwards as they continued moving. After about ten steps, she let out a little crackling squawk that sounded so much like "hmph!" that Confri couldn't help laughing after the second instance.

The humor vanished, when they stepped into one of the newer "greenhouses." A sense of recognition washed over her hard enough to threaten her balance. She barely heard Aeola ask if she was all right, as she listened to the sudden impression of a voice whispering at the back of her mind.

She had dreamed this place. She had dreamed that bench, painted bright pink, sitting next to the airlock. She had dreamed that specific tangle of blue flowering vines that arched up over the path and partially blocked the image of dozens of cocoons lying in neat rows on carefully tended beds of soil.

Acon? She shivered and held her breath. *Are you here?*

"Confri?" Aeola gently gripped her shoulder.

"I dreamed this place," she whispered. "My brother is here, isn't he?"

A choked bubble of laughter escaped her throat when her three new teammates gave her confused looks. How would they know? She didn't have her derelict ship siblings listed as family at the top of her personnel file because that listing was just for genetic or legal kinship. How could these people know that Acon was as close to a brother, genetically, as she could ever have? Their childhood bond had been equal to a twin bond.

Confri? Acon's mental voice sounded strained. It would have cracked if he had been speaking aloud. *That's it, I'm definitely going insane. All the doctors are right.*

"You're not insane, Acon," she called, pitching her voice to carry through the moist air. "We've been meeting in dreams the last few nights. This is proof."

"Confri?" His voice came from somewhere out of sight ahead of her.

She gave one last glance at her confused teammates and ran, through the archway of the trellis, down the path between the neat rows of cocoons, then taking a right turn at the first intersection. Past several walls of more climbing plants that broke up the depressing vista of rows of cocoons, dirty-greenish-silvery-white, oddly gleaming capsules of living death.

A man came out from behind the third wall up ahead of her and staggered a little when their gazes met. Confri choked on another bubble of laughter and slowed.

She would know Acon anywhere. They were the pale, thin ones in the spectrum of multiple geno-types among the derelict ship children. He stood a whole head taller than her, and wore his silvery hair cropped short, so it fuzzed around his head in the humidity. His eyes were gray-blue and hers were gray-green, but they had the same long noses and square chins.

"How did my psi get fixed?" he said, when they stopped within two meters of each other. "How am I hearing you again? I'm glad, but it doesn't make ..." Then he went even more pale and he staggered and turned, to run back the way he had come.

"It's not broken," she called after him. She glanced back over her shoulder, to see her three teammates a few dozen steps behind her. "Your bond with Merielle."

Granted, she had no way of knowing that. She suspected the bond between them had been repaired by the passenger bumping along in the bag hanging at her hip. She felt Acon's panic, and understood his fear as if the explanation was written on a screen in front of her: he feared their restored bond meant his bond with his sweetheart had broken. Or worse, she had died. Life signs were so minimal inside cocoons, it was useless to keep them hooked up to monitors. There weren't enough life-sign monitors available to service the thousands of cocoons that had been found and rescued in the decades since the Hivers had begun their attack on the Human worlds.

She came around the wall of climbing vines and nearly shrieked at the sight of Acon kneeling in front of a cocoon, with his hands on it. Then she saw a transparent sheet covered the cocoon, protecting him from those noxious filaments penetrating his flesh, entering his bloodstream, and inducing paralysis and sleeping death on him in turn.

They were late for dinner with Commodore Roop and the command team of Anwesta Station. Confri was grateful to her teammates, who insisted on staying with Acon until medics could be summoned to bring a monitor and prove that Merielle hadn't died. The commodore ended up coming down to join them.

The medics summoned her when they registered a slight uptick in brain activity within Merielle's cocoon.

"It's the egg," Dulit said, once the excitement had settled down. Most of the technicians and medics hurried away to analyze the new data streaming from the monitor attached to the cocoon.

Everyone agreed. They weren't sure how, but it was the only explanation: the egg had begun repairing Confri's bond with Acon, and through his fragile bond with Merielle had brought about some change in her condition. Whether that change was an improvement and would continue was anyone's guess.

Commodore Roop invited Acon to join them for the dinner, which turned into a long evening of theorizing and planning. She was surprised when he accepted.

I've turned into the station's ghost, or maybe a legend, he confided to Confri, as the group made their way up through the station to the dining room. *I do earn my keep. I have assigned duties, checking on the condition of the soil that feeds the cocoons. I'm not entirely pitiful. But everyone has just gotten used to me being fairly anti-social, sitting my solitary vigil with Meri and the rest of our crew.*

You're not alone anymore. She caught hold of his hand.

I know. He frowned and glanced down at the egg in its bag at her hip. *I can't begin to tell you how it feels to have you here, in my head again. And you say the egg did it? I've seen some miraculous things done by the dracs since they arrived on the station, but ... I pretty much gave up any hope they'd choose any of my crew's cocoons for tending any time soon.*

There are only so many dracs, and far too many cocoons.

How did you get an egg?

More like it got me. She grinned at him and wrinkled up her nose.

He snorted, probably as close to laughter as he had come since his ship was attacked by the Hivers.

Acon had many of his questions answered over dinner, as Commodore Roop and her team discussed all the reports generated by the appearance of the egg and the entire tangled mess on Castitarus. Confri was somewhat surprised that Granny didn't interrupt their long dinner. Then again, dracs kept popping in and out of the dining room, hovering on the periphery of the discussion for a few minutes, then popping out again. She supposed Granny was spying on them through the dracs.

Commodore Roop apologized for intruding on their privacy, then explained that she had been studying both Confri and Acon's records as soon as she learned Confri was coming to Anwesta. She had alerts established for all the derelict ship children, if they ever made contact with Acon or came to the station. She also admitted that all the foster-siblings were under constant if light observation, simply because the mystery of their origin had never been solved.

"I found it interesting that you two had a sibling bond, and the number of genetic matches, among all the ship children," the commodore said.

"One theory of our origin is that we're some kind of breeding experiment, our DNA put in a metaphorical blender to swirl together all the geno-types in the Alliance," Acon offered. "Whether we were stolen from our creators or tossed with the trash, or something happened to them and we escaped, who knows?"

"Do you want to know?" Tancredi, Commodore Roop's right-hand assistant, asked.

"Will it cause us trouble or give us comfort?" Confri shrugged. "I think that concern has been pushed down pretty far on the list."

"I agree," Roop said. "In my estimation, at least until that egg hatches and we find out what exactly we have to deal with, the highest priority is determining why and how your bond re-wove itself, if the re-established bond is affecting Dr. Merielle in her cocoon, or it's just a happy coincidence."

"Or if the presence of a numenjax egg is causing that change?" Dulit offered.

"That too." The commodore sighed. "I'm going to make a proposal that you will not be happy with," she nodded to Acon, "but I urge you to go along with me on this. You need to come under the examination of a premier master at the Academy. Several masters, working together, to fully trace your bond, the scars, the damage when the bond was broken, and just what rewove it."

"And you want us to go to Le'anka, because it would be easier to send the two of us," Confri said, "than to ask several masters, with many students, to come up here just to work with us. And rude, too." She caught hold of Acon's hand under the table and tried to send him as much comfort and sympathy as she could through their bond. It felt odd, and somehow new, to do it. When they were younger, it had been as easy as thinking.

"Exactly."

Acon flushed as everyone at the round table seemed to be focusing on him.

"I won't deny that it feels like I'd be abandoning my crew. I've had enough counselors talking to me about feeling guilty ..." He rubbed his face and sighed, and through their bond Confri felt something loosen inside him. "If understanding what's going on would help them, then ..." He nodded and tried to smile.

"We will keep a shuttle ready at all times to bring you up, the moment anything changes," the commodore promised.

~~~~~

Confri wasn't sure if they were being honored or she had underestimated just how touchy and vital the situation had become: she and Acon were welcomed as guests in Master Reydon's home. They wouldn't stay in the dormitories at the Academy, but live with their teacher and his wife, Healer Thean.

"Part of the reason," Thean explained, as she and Confri and Acon settled down for lunch in the gardens the next day, "is because Reydon and I have some experience with dracs. Especially the hatching process. And part of the reason is to protect you. Fleet and the Diplomatic Corps have been uncovering several ... well, 'spies' isn't the right term. Unethical persons who are willing to share information with anyone who asks, for a high enough price. After that debacle on Castitarus, the Maniterri insist the entire planet owes them a huge honor debt, so they want information on anyone and everyone and everything that leaves the planet."

"That explains why I get regular messages from the Maniterri ambassador," Acon said. "He's taken over the contract between Finn and Vitiarre. He's probably trying to pull the same tactics they were using on Jasper, to draft me into working for them. Give him dracs."

"You ignore him, don't you?" Thean asked.
~~~~~

"With great pleasure. Sometimes the messages from him are full of lectures over my rudeness. I figured it was safer to just ignore them, instead of responding and letting that indiferp get me into an argument that goes nowhere."

"Very wise." Her smile twitched once, making Confri guess the woman had had her own unpleasant encounters with self-righteous Maniterri.

"So they know I came from Castitarus, with an egg?" Confri guessed.

"Unfortunately. On the bright side, several people have been removed from positions giving them access to shielded communications and private information. We don't think anyone knows your identity, but it's best not to take any chances. That situation is part of why Commodore Roop sent you down here. Whoever helped some Maniterri invade Anwesta to try to capture dracs still hasn't been identified and removed from duty."

~~~~~

Acon and Confri had three days of intensive examinations, physical and mental and emotional. The teachers and technicians working with them were kind and gentle, but the whole process was exhausting. They returned to their guest quarters too tired to appreciate the luxury of their surroundings.

On a positive note, the mental exercises Master Reydon taught them measurably strengthened their regained bond, so that by the second night on Le'anka, Acon was sharing Confri's dreams and heard the voice that laughed and spoke promises and comfort. When they woke, they could never remember what they had discussed with the voice, but the impressions were strong.

On the fourth day, Master Reydon informed them at breakfast that he had received word the *Defender* was returning to Le'anka. M'kar and Thyal would be joining them, to give Confri and Acon lessons in dealing with a hatching drac. Even if what came out of the egg wasn't exactly a drac, it should still be close enough to one that the lessons and experiences passed on would help.

"That's it." He chuckled, shaking his head. "I should have thought of that sooner. They're the missing piece." He half-closed his eyes in thought while he sipped his morning tea.

"How are M'kar and our son the missing piece?" Thean asked.

"Their inexplicable bond. This inexplicably repaired bond between Confri and Acon. Multiple minds." Reydon nodded once for
~~~~~

punctuation and put the cup of tea down on the table with a click. "I should have thought of it before. The numenjax specifically mentioned the raw spot on your psi, from trauma. The trauma of your torn bond. That is what made your mind so attractive to the numenjax. You are two minds. Multiple minds bound closely together, to enable you to take the strain of communication with them."

"Just like with Thyal and M'kar, back on Castitarus," Thean said, nodding.

Confri had read every report, every offshoot speculation and theory relating to the whole concept of communication with the numenjax. She understood, and it made sense. And frightened her a little. What kind of a mind did the occupant of the egg possess, and just how aware was he, how active was his mental powers, that he could find a multiple mind, even as damaged as her bond was with Acon, to latch onto when he hatched?

Looking at the growing frown lines in Acon's forehead and around his mouth, her brother didn't understand. He probably didn't know those details of the mission to Castitarus. That morning, instead of taking more tests and learning new mental exercises, she and Acon went over the mission logs and reports and learned everything they could about dracs, the ceramic tablets on Draxonis, and the numenjax.

~~~~~

M'kar and Thyal arrived that afternoon, and both were surprised enough by the sight of the egg Confri pulled out of the pouch hanging at her hip, it worried her. Then she had to laugh, when they explained that the egg was much larger, nearly half again as large, as any drac egg they had seen.

"I thought I was imagining it," she said, to explain her laughter. "I thought this thing was getting larger and heavier ... well, he does eat an awful lot."

"That means the shell has to stay soft, or at least soft enough to keep expanding to hold whoever is inside," M'kar mused. "So how much larger is he going to get? What if the shell doesn't go crystalline like it does for dracs, just before hatching?"

Thyal tapped the egg. The sound was more a thud like hitting a thick piece of wood than the crackle or chime that had been described just before a drac shell shattered into dust.

"So ... basically we won't know it's going to happen until it starts
~~~~~

to happen?" Acon said.

They discussed what they knew, and what they didn't know, and in the end had to agree. There were preparations that could be made, though, based on the experiences of the crew of the *Defender*, and what Dulit, Flinders and Aeola had undergone. First was to be ready to physically collapse, while resisting the mental "suckage" that occurred when the hatchling latched onto the adopted parent's mind. There would be several hours of sleep while the bonding occurred, then both Humans and hatchling would wake starving, and the battle to impose discipline and order in the hungry young mind would commence.

Confri and Acon needed to strengthen their unity of mind, and practice working together, in preparation for the hatching, when they would get the full force of the numenjax mind. They could only theorize that both of them would be caught up in the bond. M'kar and Thyal could both laugh at the mental "suckage" they experienced with their newborn dracs, but Confri and Acon were both apprehensive at how much worse it would be for them with a numenjax. Dracs were, after all, shrunken versions of numenjax, everything dialed down to just a fraction of the size and strength and intelligence.

~~~~~

Three days later, the four were in the gardens, discussing the possibility of a trip up to Anwesta, to check a theory. Merielle's cocoon was still generating slightly stronger brain activity than all the other cocoons in Anwesta. Master Reydon had theorized that distance prohibited any effect from the strengthening bond between Acon and Confri. If they and the egg returned to Anwesta, would there be some change in Merielle when they got closer to her cocoon? And just how close did they need to be?

A chiming crack broke through the pause in the discussion. Barroo and Infrenx let out loud, prolonged cries and leaped up from M'kar and Thyal's shoulders, to hover in wide circles over the egg. It sat in its usual spot, in a puddle of food pellets, in the sunshine, on a cushion.

The voice that had wept and chattered and laughed in Confri's dreams for so long now spoke, but the words weren't clear. Confri understood anyway.

"He's coming," she said.

The egg cracked, with another loud chime. It wobbled enough
~~~~~

to move aside some of the food pellets. Confri had a vision of the egg rolling off the cushion, onto the paving tiles.

"What do I do?"

"He's going to be confused, and probably cold, and desperate for something familiar." Thyal gave her an encouraging smile. "You're already familiar with each other, so that should help. I guess you should just be ready to catch him when he pops out."

Confri muffled a squeak of sudden fear. She had an awful image of the hatchling popping out of the egg, falling the to the paving tiles, and breaking something vital. She hurried to get on her knees in front of the cushion. Acon hurried to kneel facing her, with the cushion and the egg between them.

Barroo and Infrenx popped out. That was a relief. Their cries were just a half-step sharp, and irritating. She did not need distraction right now.

Dozens of black crack lines spread through the mottled, jewel-toned shell. Another black line zigged through the shell with a pinging sound.

You have incredible timing, you know that?

A whisper of laughter answered her.

Maybe this won't be as bad as we feared? Acon reached across the egg and caught hold of her hands.

I have no idea. At least I'm not alone in here. Wherever here is.

Then she was somehow inside the egg, looking through the cracks, seeing herself and Acon. She hovered between curiosity, wanting to get out, and a strange reluctance to leave what was familiar and enclosed and safe.

But she had a job to do and the time had come to do it.

"He has a job to do," she whispered.

"He was sent," Acon said, nearly at the same time.

The cracks multiplied and the shell shattered into fragments, not the expected dust, exploding outward. Confri no longer looked out, but looked in. At gossamer shifting panels of gold and crimson, with veins of emerald.

"Hello," she whispered, and tugged free of her brother's grip to lean over the egg. More pieces fell away from the sides. The gossamer unfolded. Wings. Hands trembling, she reached in, trying to slide her fingers down between the shell and the neatly coiled shape. She laughed at the warmth and smoothness.

"You expected it to be slimy, didn't you?" Acon said. She stuck her tongue out at him and he let out a bark of laughter.

A trilling started out soft and low, then rose in pitch and volume, turning into a triumphant chortle as the numenjax's long, triangular head emerged from the cover of its wings wrapped around itself. Eyes like sapphires stared into Confri's. She held her breath, braced for the brain "suckage" to start.

Hello. The voice sounded soft, warm, tentative, but not infantile.

Confri wasn't sure why she expected to hear a baby voice. *Are you hungry? Are you cold? Are you all right?*

Hungry. Cold. Hold me?

With a crooning moan, Confri slid her hands under the unfolding, smooth, soft hide and elegant bone, somehow knowing just how to avoid tangling in the delicate wings. She scooped the numenjax up and against her chest, so his head rested on her shoulder.

Tired. He let out a happy-sounding sigh and closed all those eyelids.

The newborn numenjax was larger than Barroo and Infrenx, who popped back in and settled down on the pavement, eyes swirling with multiple colors. They let out chirps and trills of excitement.

"Why isn't she flat on her back yet?" Thyal whispered.

"He doesn't need me to control him and keep him from sucking my brain dry." Confri shivered a little, knowing part of the answer, or at least the certainty of it, came from Jax. She laughed. He had named himself, or let her name him. "His name is Jax. He's here to help us."

"Help us how?" M'kar said.

"I'm not sure yet," Acon said.

Since neither Acon nor Confri were physically or mentally incapacitated, they decided to go into the house to find food to feed the newborn. Jax trilled happily at the mention of food. Thyal called ahead to his parents. Some food prepared in anticipation of need was quickly heated, and they gathered around the table in the kitchen. Jax opened his eyes, sniffing, and wriggling a little like an eager child. Confri's stomach pinched with hunger. Acon laughed and admitted he felt Jax's hunger, too. She followed her nose, obeying the impressions Jax shared with her, and scooped up a basket of fresh bread, dripping with chunks of fruit preserves. She tore it into small pieces. Those went down Jax's throat rapidly, with an odd sense of elegance. That was followed by a bowl of cold chopped soogi fowl.

The entire experience was an odd mixture of satisfying and disappointing, relief and curiosity. Confri and Acon were both relieved to be spared the "suckage," and the exhaustion. Yet they both had to admit, when they thought about it later, they had looked forward to the sense of discovery and the challenge of being parents to the young mind.

"The problem is that he's been aware this whole time, learning, and teaching us a little. We just haven't been conscious of it," Acon summed up for them, when they tried to explain what they felt.

"That's probably part of this job he was sent to do," M'kar said. "When do we start learning what he came for?"

No one had an answer for that, because Jax had eaten until his stomach was round and hard, then fell asleep with a contented burp. At least in that area, he was like newborn dracs.

~~~~~

Confri realized quickly that the disappointment she felt, under all her relief, came from realizing that she had been thinking of Jax as her child. He wasn't. Not like the dracs were children to Dulit, Flinders, and Aeola.

That was made abundantly clear when Jax woke up from his post-gorge nap and asked to go up to Anwesta. Not in words, this time, but images of the medical station, inside and outside. Acon received the same message.

There was no delay, because after all, Commodore Roop had promised a shuttle would be waiting if Acon ever needed to return to the station and to the greenhouse and Merielle. The request for the flight up to Anwesta was granted quickly, without any trouble. Except when the communication officer passed on Dulit's warning: *Granny's going to throw a hissy.*

Confri knew she was being nasty, but she looked forward to the silver drac's dismay and consternation when she encountered the baby numenjax.

Jax purred happily and curled up onto his perch on Confri's shoulder when they left Reydon and Thean's house. Somehow, he managed to make himself look smaller. The walk to the spaceport didn't garner as many second looks and stares and comments from the people they passed as she had feared. Surely the people at the Academy couldn't be used to dracs in large enough numbers to be an ordinary occurrence. She wondered if Jax had any special mental
~~~~~

abilities, like influencing people not to see or notice him. She didn't ask, but when she had that thought, Jax's happy purr turned into a trill of laughter for a moment or two. She detected a note of smugness.

Where were you when I needed to be invisible, growing up?

That got another trill. She decided maybe she wasn't quite so disappointed that she didn't have a baby to teach and guide. This was more like having a playmate, or a fellow adventurer.

Everyone in the shuttle was in a good mood until the shuttle docked with Anwesta. Dulit and Flinders promised to meet them. They couldn't promise that Granny or her spies wouldn't guess something was happening, and come interfere.

The moment they stepped through the hatch, everyone immediately went on alert. Infrenx and Barroo rose from their parents' shoulders and moved in front of them. Confri had an immediate mental image of guards preparing to deflect an attack.

Poki popped in a moment later, then Dulit came around a bend in the corridor outside the shuttle bay. He looked a little winded, like he had run. No sign of Granny yet. Poki came within arm's reach of Jax and they both stretched their necks out, nearly touching noses. She nodded, he nodded, and she let out a happy chirp and settled on Dulit's shoulder.

He's keeping them away, isn't he? Acon asked.

She nodded and reached up to stroke Jax's neck. *Thanks.*

Jax purred louder.

They walked down two corridors, headed for Commodore Roop's office, to report to her. They came to a column in the station with six intersecting corridors and three lift tubes, and paused to wait for a lift to arrive. Jax stiffened and raised his head. He uncoiled from Confri's shoulders, spread his wings, and darted down the corridor to the left. A heartbeat later, the other dracs followed. They were silent.

Silent dracs had to mean something important. Possibly frightening. Serious, at the very least.

Confri ran after Jax. Acon caught up with her in a few steps, and she heard several sets of running feet behind them. Station personnel were standing still, looking down the corridor when Confri reached them, all in the direction of Jax's path. She supposed it was good that no alarms had been raised. Maybe everyone was so used to dracs on board the station, they didn't panic, even when they didn't recognize the larger drac that raced down the curving corridor?

They came to another column and the dracs and Jax paused a moment. Confri stumbled when Jax hovered, looking back at her, then darted out one taloned forepaw to press the controls for the lift. A moment later, he popped out. So, now she knew he could teleport. A moment later, all the dracs vanished as well. The lift car doors opened. She threw herself in. Fortunately, no one was already in there. Acon followed. M'kar caught up with them. The doors closed. Acon hit the command to take them up to the right level for Merielle's greenhouse.

Confri nearly laughed, as she realized she had wasted a lot of time studying how to be a drac parent. Jax was clearly in control, not even a day old. Maybe he had been in control since his egg was deposited in the cargo bin. Maybe he had been the voice whispering at the back of her mind, bringing her to the shuttle bay. He made her find him, and started them down the long road to here.

The lift door hissed open. Double doors were open only a few steps down the corridor, and a smell of damp soil and green growing things and the sweet, overwhelming aroma of cocoons, the signature stink of Hivers, spilled out of the doors to greet them.

Two steps into the greenhouse, lights flashed, red and yellow, and alarm sirens wailed. Suddenly personnel in gray medical jumpsuits came from all directions. Confri felt a yank, like someone had tied a thread around her brain and pulled. She followed it, down paths between long plots of moist soil with neat rows of cocoons. The invisible mental thread led her to intersect with the medics, directly underneath the flashing lights and the source of the siren. She pushed through the people who came to a sudden stop and formed a wall around a plot of soil. The dracs hovered overhead, but not Jax.

Acon let out a moan that told her just where they were, even before she recognized the neat markers on the edge of the pavement. They had returned to Merielle's cocoon.

Confri stumbled down into the soil, and nearly fell forward onto the cocoon where Jax had spread himself full length. His forelegs and hind legs embraced the cocoon, and his wings extended as if warding everyone away. His tail twitched, like he was brushing away irritating insects. Or maybe he was just irritated, period. Confri caught her balance and clenched her fists. She itched all over at the thought of nearly touching that cocoon. She had heard horror stories of the damage done to people who touched the cocoons with their bare hands.

"Doubled brainwave activity," a deep-voiced man said from the other side of the cocoon. He stood looking down at Jax, and waved a large, complicated-looking medical scanner. Awe spread over his face along with the multi-colored lights from the scanner.

"I think we just figured out why Jax chose you," M'kar said, as she wedged her way through the gathering crowd to reach Confri's side.

Overhead, the dracs trilled, and more dracs from Anwesta joined them. Jax raised his head and trilled laughter. Confri wrapped her arms around herself, trembling a little, knots of tension loosening throughout her body. This was something even more important and helpful and good than finding a new Chute or understanding Gates. This was giving lives back to people who had been sleeping, prisoners of cocoons, for decades. Jax was only one numenjax and she had no way of knowing how long it would take for him to awaken someone who had been sleeping for two years now. But she couldn't, she wouldn't let herself be overwhelmed by the numbers and the odds.

Hope had come to Anwesta, and she and Acon had been chosen to pair with Jax and be part of it.

End

ICE DRAGON
By James K. Bowers

Within her cave of crystal, her lair of evergleams,
    The dragon slept, eyes tight-closed, dreaming her icy dreams.
Quite near there stood the castle, great bastion of the north,
    Yet home for highborn cowards from which no knights rode
forth.
On that moonless winter night a nameless warrior came
    To test his wits and weapons, no wish for wealth or fame.
"If a quest is what you seek," the haughty baron said,
    "Then slay the Ice-cave dragon, and bring to me its head!"
Frost demons danced wicked-white and heartless windwraiths
wailed.
    Through it all the warrior trudged and not one footstep failed.
Into her lair he entered, then blundered through the maze;
    He came upon her chamber -- then met the dragon's gaze.
Cold eyes of northwind blue and scales pure diamond white,
    A beast of tooth and talon, with wings too small for flight,
A nameless, godless terror of countless wicked years,
    Thirty yards from tip to tip -- creature of nightmare fears.
In words as cold as frozen steel, in phrases of deep jet,
    The dragon hissed her challenge (or, perhaps, a timeworn
threat):
"Puny man with worthless shield and single, tiny claw,
    Give your life to me this night -- my armor has no flaw."
Then she breathed a glass shard gust, thinking his fate was sealed.
    The man but staggered backward and blocked it with his shield.
Then with claws as cold as death, the warrior she engaged.
    Wounds she dealt, but none she took, yet on the battle raged.
Losing hope, still on he fought against the reptile's bulk,
    Soaking in his own red blood, his shield a battered hulk.
Fearing death, the warrior cried, "You shall bleed, at least!"
    His sword sang once, then twice, then sank into the beast.
The dragon shrieked and shuddered, in pain December deep,

And from the wyrm's white belly quicksilver blood did seep.
Her crystal scales had lost their gleam; her azure eyes were dim;
    He thought the dragon had expired, but then -- it spoke to him:
"Little man, my thanks are yours -- you end this curse on me.
    Many live in fear of death, but death shall set me free.
I have fought uncounted foes and all have died in vain --
    By the nature of my curse: to slay and not be slain.
Still I had just one small hope; and now it comes to pass --
    Blessed to fall before the man with heart not steel, but glass."
Arctic winds and frozen mists escaped from dragonsbreath;
    One last heave of massive chest and then she welcomed death.
His eyes grew wide in wonder as flesh replaced wyrmhide,
    A maiden, cold and lifeless, lay where the dragon died.
Within her cave of crystal he cried his bitter tears,
    And softly spoke in whispers some words for Sorrow's ears.
Into his arms he took her and wrapped her in his cloak,
    Then lifted her lifeless form; his spirit all but broke.
Across his weary shoulder she lay in endless sleep --
    A burden he would carry back to the baron's keep.
Step by aching step he fought through drifts waist deep and more;
    In sorrow he forged onward, though at him cold winds tore.
Into the keep he entered, with pale and morbid prize,
    And then into the throne room with tears that blurred his eyes.
The baron sat proud and high, with knights arrayed by rank,
    Attended by young damsels who served the wine they drank.
"And now arrives our hero," spoke the baron in delight.
    "Pray tell us of the dragon, and valor as a knight!"
The room was filled with silence, the feast forgotten now;
    All eyes were on the warrior as anguish creased his brow.
Said he, "Here is your dragon," and lightly brushed her hair.
    Gently then he laid her down and cried, "Does no one care?"
The baron blinked and stammered, and then just looked away;
    No tears were shed by damsels; the knights had naught to say.
Then to the floor he dropped his sword and left it where it lay.
    He eyed the court in pity, then turned and walked away.
Yet unclaimed the sword remains within that gloomy hall --
    None dare touch that fateful blade, that curse upon them all...

Written in 1986 and published in Kankakee Community College's
The Prairie Fire, 1989.